# gr

/groōmed/ *verb (past tense)*

To prepare or train (someone) for a particular purpose or activity.

Renee,
May you find humor & humility in the messiness of life.
Jody Paschal

# Groomed

Jody Paschal

Published by Paschal's Prose, 2024.

This is a work of fiction. Similarities to real people, places, or events are entirely coincidental.

GROOMED

**First edition. November 29, 2024.**



ISBN: 979-8227679055

Written by Jody Paschal.

Thank you to the individuals and figments of my imagination who lent their voices to creating this story. You've uncovered uncomfortable truths and empowered strength, courage, and giggles that needed release. I'm forever grateful for the journey.

# Introduction

## Hindsight, 2020 and Planet of the Aint's

The Roaring 20s. The sound of fury made the year Mother Nature and Father Time said, "fuck humanity!" and exercised self-care. Their sabbatical marked 2020 as the year from hell—ushering in a global pandemic, the deaths of countless legends, and the Black Lives Matter and Me Too movements. It's also the year I turned 50 and developed a 20/20 vision that finally allowed me to see myself.

My name is Myles Gunn. My friends call me Mylo. I'm an average Joe who loves Jesus, cussing, coffee, comedy, music, and never being alone with my thoughts for too long. To say the year 2020 fucked me all the way up would be a ginormous understatement.

For one, quarantine felt like fighting in hell with a squirt gun. It was the Dark Ages. Some jailhouse rock meets sign of the times shit. A time when professional felt personal and personal was having a motherfucking identity crisis. The constant loop of introspection, doom, regret, fear, and confinement was a low-rent nightmare occupying every conscious and unconscious thought in my head. I spent hours listening to myself breathe in my mask while watching the world turn into a literal dumpster fire on CNN. It was A LOT.

Don't get me wrong, I'm a loner. But this time alone was different. The irony of hindsight and 2020. I think that was the hardest part. Like I said before, I don't sit well with my thoughts for too long.

Luckily, I didn't have to spend all of lockdown at home driving my wife, Traci, nuts. I work as a facilities manager for a government contractor and am a professional church musician. So when lockdown happened, I became an essential worker and unemployed simultaneously. In other words, I was on the front lines the day the music died. Churches were closed, and as a facilities manager, being in the office daily was "business as usual."

But the office was eerie. Our space only housed 30 employees. And the only peeps around during the pandemic were me, our cleaning lady Petra, and Chris, our IT support specialist. We were the three musketeers, safeguarding printer ink and paper clips in the name of capitalism. I felt like Will Smith in *I Am Legend*. Except I was wishing Scotty would beam me up.

Speaking of alien encounters, let me tell you about the day of reckoning that led me here. It was I Am Legend-ary, riddled with ET references and close encounters of the strangest kind.

It all started with Petra's arrival at the office. But first, here's a little backstory on Petra...

As I said, Petra's the cleaning lady for our building. She's a loud, gossipy, Spanglish-speaking Honduran with a gigantic heart. I'm convinced she was an airhorn with an inferiority complex in a previous life. Petra's what you'd call a jealous wallflower. An attention whore with a temper who doesn't want to be seen. Which is why being a cleaner is the perfect day job for her.

As I mentioned earlier, English isn't Petra's first language. And she's knighted me as her linguistics sounding board since she's obsessed with speaking like *'a respectable white woman'* instead of the nosy and brash drama queen she is. Petra's drama meter was set to extra zesty on this particular Thursday. She got off the elevator, schlepping a bike with a wicker basket on the handles, wearing a blanket-like shawl over her head and a hefty scowl across her brow.

"Jefe! Ay Dios mío! The chickens are bringing the cold today!" she bellowed through her mask.

"Hi, Petra. You mean the hawk is out?" I responded.

Petra snapped, "Yes, Jefe. That's what I say. Your ears on vacation from the cold or something? You don't have the Corona beer, do you?"

I laugh-talked, "No, Petra. My ears are fine, and I don't have the damn Coronavirus. So exhale and smile before your frown lines freeze in place. I left my chisel and patience at home."

Petra pulled down her mask and gave me a megawatt smile, "Why you so estricto, Jefe? Here!" She handed me a pack of Reese's Pieces. I thanked her and suddenly had the urge to phone home.

A few minutes after my encounter with Petra, our IT guy, Chris, appeared. Chris is a nerd with nerve—your stereotypical awkward, self-centered, know-it-all techie with the tact of an over-opinionated five-year-old. I call him Pinky and the Brain because he tells me daily that he's planning to take over a company in the future. I nod and stay on his good side if it ever happens.

A few months before the pandemic hit, Chris confided he didn't like how he looked and felt uncomfortable in his skin. He's racially and sexually ambiguous and has been dropping me crumbs about his life-long identity crisis for the past two years. So I was happy he felt comfortable coming clean with me. That heart-to-heart chat kinda bonded us as friends. We've been cool ever since.

Chris has been using the empty office as an opportunity to discover his personal style. He's appointed Petra and me as judges for his project runway, and this particular week, he was experimenting with masks. Chris showed up that day wearing a Stormtrooper mask with an n95 mask over it. He claims he was having a bad hair day. Petra and I gave him a double thumbs down and an eye roll for emphasis.

Petra circled back to my desk around lunchtime with her cell phone in hand. "Jefe, look at this!" She shoved her phone in my face.

"I failed my test yesterday." Petra was taking ESL classes online and gave me weekly progress reports.

"This is no bueno. You help me do better, yes? My English is better when I talk to you. So you have to help me more. My therapist tell me that is good for me, Jefe."

I raised my eyebrow "Wait, therapist? When did you start seeing a therapist?"

Petra responded, "I no tell you? I go to therapy three times now! Very nice lady. I want to talk like her."

"That's nice, Petra. What made you decide to go to therapy? Everything okay?" I asked.

Petra furrowed her brow "Remember last month I tell you I argue with my son about his controladora girlfriend? Well, he tell me I'm biplar and need to be shrunk back to normal. So I go online and find a shrink because I no want to be biplar. My husband call me honey, I shrunk the loca now."

Petra didn't even wait for me to respond. She spun around on her hot pink Crocs and headed down the hall, garbage bags flailing from her back pocket. I whispered, "space cadet," and shook my head. It took me another 10 minutes to figure out that biplar meant bipolar.

"Shit, I'm probably the one who needs to be shrunk. Maybe I'll ask Petra to take me to her leader." I went back to eating my lunch.

Halfway through my salad, my cell phone rang. "Awwh, hell!" It was my pain in my ass friend, Calvin. Where do I even start with him? I've known Calvin since Christ was a child. We grew up together and he's like a bad habit I've never been able to shake. He's a baby daddy with issues and an obsessive appetite for self-sabotage. He knows better but doesn't do better and has been in and out of prison for a total of 10 years. Not for any violent crimes or misdemeanors, mind you. He's continually been locked up for child support evasion and a horrible pull-out game. I answered the call.

"Man, what you doing?" Calvin barked.

I responded, "Fool, I'm at work. What YOU doing?"

Calvin answered, "You at work, huh? That's what's up! Man, I just finished breaking up a fight between two rats. You know I don't allow violence in my house."

I busted out laughing. Calvin hung up. Typical Calvin. He'll call back.

It was quiet now, and my mind was racing again. Hearing from Calvin always transported me to my past life. He reminded me of youth, naiveté, and poor choices, so I rarely talk to Calvin. Thankfully, our conversations never last that long.

I try not to think about it. The mistake that snatched my youth. I'd bounced back and made a success of myself. I'm happy, healthy, and about to turn 50. I should be seeing the light, not ruminating in darkness. I tell you, hindsight and 2020 is a serious mind fuck.

I'd managed to avoid doom watching CNN for most of the day. But the day had already morphed into a telenovela of The Young and the Chestless. So, I decided to play news roulette and turned the volume up on the next story segment.

*"The GOP culture war continues. With Republicans shining a spotlight on sexual grooming and anti-gay legislation, arguments are swirling over which political party has the most pedophiles. Well, one Republican congresswoman's name is trending at the top of that list. Kentucky Representative Jackie Flowers' young husband is raising some SERIOUS questions. Here's her engagement announcement from 2014. And no, that's not her son. She's nearly two decades older than her husband, Mike, and they were engaged before he graduated college. The two reportedly met when he was in high school, where Flowers served as a board chair. At the time of their meeting, it was reported that she was 35 and he was 16. In a speech at a Young Business Leaders of America event, Mike praised Flowers for granting him a scholarship from her family that changed his life. Well, it appears she gave him more than that. She served as his mentor and personal coach and ensured he never had to have a job while pursuing his studies. Perhaps..."*

I turned off the TV and stared for a moment. I couldn't focus and was sweating. My hands were trembling. I looked up and noticed Petra and Chris were in the room with me. Their presence calmed me a bit.

The two of them were talking, but their voices were background noise. I grabbed my phone and googled *"sexual grooming."* My only context with the phrase was the current political rhetoric that teachers who mention sexual orientation are "grooming" kids to be gay. I'd never heard the phrase applied to the Mrs. Robinsons of the world. Or me. I frantically read through the search results...

*Intentional manipulation.*

*Predatory behavior for personal gain.*

*Emotional blackmail.*

*Robbery.*

*Seduce, influence, dominate...*

*Victims are GROOMED.*

Wait, this can't be me.

"Mylo! Mylo! Earth to Mylo!!!" Chris yelled and shook my shoulder. The sight of his Stormtrooper mask shook me out of my stupor.

I shouted, "Got damn! Stop shaking me, you little fucker! I feel like I'm on one of those horrible amusement park rides that make you hurl."

Chris backed up with a concerned look. "Dude, are you okay? You're sweating, and your hands are shaking. You need some water? Should I call your wife?"

"Nah, no need to call Traci and disturb the peace at home. I'm fine." I huffed. "Did you see that story about the lady politician marrying that young kid?" I asked.

Petra responded, "Yes, Jefe. They make the big deal. When woman chase the tiger, she no good. When old man chase young girl, they tell him he wear nice suit for a priest."

"The women are called cougars, not tigers, Petra." I corrected.

"And my first wife was one. Well, I thought she was one. According to my Google search, I was like that 16-year-old high school kid who was groomed. My first wife groomed me." Saying the words made me lightheaded.

"Shit! You got married at 16? That's fucked up!" Chris hollered.

"No, dumbass. I got married at 20. We started dating when I was 17. She was 25. I can't believe I took a grown-ass woman to my senior prom!" I declared.

Chris asked, "How was that, dude?"

I responded, "Awkward as fuck. She was older than my English teacher who chaperoned."

We all chuckled at that, and then there was an awkward silence. Petra was scowling and looking straight through me. I could see the wheels spinning in her head.

"Jefe," she said. "I so sorry what I say before. Cougars should not eat alive nice man like you. I see now it scramble your cabeza. You need to write down what happened. That's what my therapist tell me to do. Talk to the paper. It make your mind slow down so you don't be biplar. I don't want you to be biplar, Jefe."

Petra hugged me then shoved me out of the way to empty my trash. She was right. I needed to write down the experience with my first marriage. Transfer my thoughts outside my head so I can get some peace...

I started preparing to close up shop for the day. My day on Planet of the Aints had come full circle: biplar bikes, Reese's Pieces, Stormtroopers, rat rage, and a vocabulary aha moment. Scotty had finally beamed me up. I closed out the Google search on my phone and opened my Amazon account to purchase a journal.

*******************************************************************************

# PART 1

## The Wonder Years

# The Declaration of Independence

High School. The battleground of peer pressure, angst, identity crisis, and hormones that pilots us to the ultimate falsehood of freedom – Adulthood. You're operating in a constant state of confusion and fight-or-flight social anxiety. Carefully curating the perfect war crimes between classes to lose your innocence and win your independence after school. Because that's where the *REAL* freedom exists. At the time, you think the war games are about accumulating cool points and bragging rights. But you later realize the real end game is discovering what makes you loveable.

The U.S. declared its independence in 1776. Mine started in the fall of 1987. I was 17 years old and in my second year playing organ for a local Baptist church. I was living my dream as a paid musician for one of the largest Black churches in Buffalo. The church had just celebrated its choirs' anniversary (which consisted of seven choirs). I played for each choir's performance. So I was popular, on top of the world, and enjoying every ounce of the attention I was receiving. That was until my girlfriend, Peaches, decided to bust my bubble.

Peaches was my high school sweetheart. We'd been dating off and on for four years. She was a year older than me and attended a different high school. I thought Peaches was perfect because my Dad always told me, "A peach a day keeps the heartache at bay." But at that time, Peaches and I were in an argument. I'd caught her in a lie and discovered she'd been cheating on me. Because, inside every peach, there's a stone. And hers hung like a weight anchored to my waist. Because of the argument, Peaches decided not to attend the concert last minute. I was a wreck and under a lot of stress trying to navigate my trust issues with Peaches. A month prior, I went on a popcorn and water diet and shed 35 pounds in three weeks. I was thin, depressed, and easy prey for a Groomer with small standards and an appetite for low-hanging fruit.

My groomer's sister Brenda was in the sanctuary choir and we ran in the same music circles. Brenda was six years older than me, and we were friends. No hanky panky or anything like that. Brenda weighed 350 pounds at the time. And if you knew me, you'd understand that heavy-duty beauty is a deal breaker for me. Don't get me wrong. I won't shy away from a big butt and a smile or tatas with cups that runneth over. But Lane Bryant girls do absolutely NOTHING for me. Anyway, I'd told Brenda about Peaches cheating on me and how completely crushed I was since it wasn't Peaches' first indiscretion. Brenda listened attentively, told me I had a lot to offer, and assured me everything would work out. Then, she excused herself to greet some of the other congregants.

After the concert, me and my best friend at the time, Rick Ramsey, were taking in congratulations when Brenda called us over to introduce me to her sister April. April was absolutely beautiful. First string. Not second generation. She dressed youthfully yet conservatively, with shoulder-length hair, a Cindy Crawford mole above her lip, and designer glasses. I was completely smitten. She was a Rolls Royce compared to Peaches, who was my Cadillac. April and I exchanged pleasantries, then she invited me and Rick to her apartment that evening with Brenda. We eagerly accepted, then returned to collecting our compliments as we exited the church.

I drove Rick and I to April's apartment around 7 pm. April's other sister Pam was already there with a young boy who sang tenor in our youth choir. It was officially a party. Rick, Choir Boy, and I exchanged looks and dapped each other up. We were in grown folks' business and ready to close some deals.

April had a whole feast prepared for us. Meatloaf, rice, gravy, tossed salad, rolls and red Kool-Aid. We all ate, laughed, and got acquainted. Everyone was paired up. Pam and Choir Boy claimed their corner, Brenda and Rick were on one couch, and April and I were on another. About an hour after dinner, Pam made her move on Choir Boy, Brenda was all over Rick, and April was all over me. Rick and I stayed until at least 3 am. Choir Boy had a curfew and left around 10 pm. Mind you, this was a Sunday. I had my car, so I dropped Rick off at his house in the city and then made the 40-minute drive home.

I didn't sleep at all and got up the next day in a daze. I listened to the song *Natural High* by the R&B group Bloodstone on repeat as I drove to school. I was in a strange euphoria of adrenaline, digestion, hormones, and disbelief. At the time, I didn't know how old April was, but I had a hunch she was a lot older than me since she had her own apartment. In hindsight, it all makes sense now. This was a different kind of family affair. April, Brenda, and Pam had been preparing their pick and roll to groom us from the start. A whole meal was ready for young teenage boys who ate like horses. And our adolescent naiveté had been plated for dessert. A family that preys together...

I couldn't believe that an older woman was interested in me. April was everything and more than I'd ever dreamed of. We didn't have sex, but we'd locked lips for hours, so you might as well say we'd had intercourse. I didn't tell any of my friends at school. I wanted to keep it to myself. Besides, I hadn't told Peaches yet.

I figured I'd call Peaches after school and let her feel the anguish I'd felt each time she'd cheated on me. However, the Grapes (in this case, Peaches) of Wrath already awaited me when I got home. Peaches had left 22 messages on my answering machine. I thought my Mom was gonna kill me because my phone was ringing so much.

I called Peaches and could barely get a word in. She cussed me ALL the way out! And she didn't cuss on the regular. It was funny but not a laughing matter. She was extremely hurt. But I absolutely. did. not. care. I was happy to hear her hurt like I had countless times before. I felt bad for her. Yet in the back of my mind, I was like, "That's what you get, Peaches! You made me cry, and you laughed in my face in front of everybody, and now it's your turn!" She kept asking where I was all night. I kept telling her I was at Rick's house. She said I was lying because her cousin took her to Rick's house, and his dad said he hadn't seen him all day. I let her keep ranting then I told her we could chat more the next day.

After Peaches and I hung up, I called April and told her everything. April consoled me, saying that these things happen and I needed to move on and get out there. That made me feel better. We talked for about twenty minutes before she returned to work. I told April I'd call her the next day.

I took the bus to school the next day. Peaches picked me up after school and gave me a ride home. The look on her face let me know she was hotter than fish grease. The car was silent all the way to my house. When we arrived, I thanked Peaches for the ride and told her I needed to do some homework and practice the piano. She jumped out of the car and demanded we talk. We went inside the house, and I led her downstairs to the basement. I could tell she was hurt, so I hugged her. Things got hot and heavy, and we began having sex. Afterward, she asked, "Now what?"

"It's over. For good." I said with a confidence that scared me.

I saw her temple twitch. Peaches snatched away from me and stood up.

"Fuck you, Mylo!" she screamed. Peaches whole body was trembling. When my emotion didn't change, she began pleading with me. You know the spiel... I'll change. I'm sorry for all I've put you through... blah, blah, yada, yada. But I was mentally checked out. She asked me if I was seeing someone else. I gave her a silent half-smile and watched her marinate in hurt. I know it sounds terrible, but that moment felt even better than the sex we'd just had. Peaches got dressed, looked at me coldly, and said something I'll never forget. "You'll never find anybody better than me, EVER!!" There she was. The REAL Peaches. The bully who'd made me doubt my worth. Her words confirmed that it was over, and it was time for me to move on. In the kindest way I could muster, I thanked Peaches for our four-year relationship. I thanked her for what we'd taught each other and emphasized that I would never forget it. BUT. IT. WAS. OVER. I kissed her cheek and opened the door for her. She shot me a look that should have scorched my soul. Instead, I watched Peaches peel out of the driveway, relieved. I was finally free.

Once again, I called April and told her everything. April told me I did the right thing and should come over to her place on Friday at 8 pm.

## The Parent Trap

You're probably wondering where my parents were during the clusterfuck unfolding in my so-called life. Well, my parents' relationship was an interesting dynamic, to say the least. If you think my relationships were fucked up, my parents were hold my beer personified.

Drama was a central character in my family story. My early years were marked by dysfunction, volatility, disengagement, and divorce. Daphne and Myles Gunn, Sr. divorced when I was five, and Dad didn't actively support my upbringing. The divorce was collateral damage from years of my Dad's transgressions. Myles Gunn, Sr. was a gifted preacher, womanizer, abuser, and high-functioning alcoholic. In hindsight, I believe he was never prepared for the shotgun life he fell into. You see, my mom was a virgin when she and my dad met. They got pregnant the first time they had sex. And since my dad was a preacher, marriage was their only answer. An answer my Dad could never fully accept. So alcohol, women, and conflict deflected the struggle between the angel and devil tormenting his conscience.

To say I was ANGRY when my Dad left would be a gross understatement. I felt like he gave up. Didn't try hard enough. Abandoned his family for a damn bottle and some snatch. My Mom had to work doubles all the time to keep everything afloat. On top of that, she suffered severely from diabetes and high blood pressure. I had to take care of my Mom and watched her struggle. I became the man of the house before I learned to ride a bike. And it was all Big Myles' fault. That's why I adopted the nickname Mylo. I wanted to disengage from the character markers attached to my Dad's name and my Mother's suffering. I DIDN'T WANT TO BE LIKE HIM!!!!!

So the shit show unraveling in my love life was an emotional inheritance. One that made me the perfect prototype for being groomed.

Although I'd been out all night playing tonsil hockey and melon ball with April, my Mom didn't immediately say anything about it to me. My Mom, Daphne Gunn, was a juvenile detention counselor and the perfect combination of no-nonsense and chill. I'd started having sex really young, and at 15, Daphne left a jumbo box of condoms on my dresser and recited the mantra from the black mama handbook, "*Don't go bringing no babies into this house while you're still a baby yourself!*" She disclosed she knew I was sexually active and explained all of the precautions. Daphne made it clear I could always talk to her about sex or anything at any time. She told me I was the most important person in the world to her and that she'd always stop and listen to me. I guess she knew I was a really responsible young man. So, being out all night didn't trip off her Spidey senses. At least that's what I thought. Little did I know, my Mom knew everything. She'd allowed me to do my thing and waited for me to tell her (which I finally did weeks later). But more about that in a bit.

Since the relationship with my Dad was every other weekend and whenever the spirit led, I became one of the village people. Not of the YMCA persuasion but of the "it takes a village to raise a child" philosophy. And trust me, I was a handful. My male influences mainly came from the community of church musicians who tried to steer me in the right direction musically and as a man. One of those influences was Marcus Booth. Marcus was one of the toughest organists in the area. Musically, I wanted to be just like him. Personally, Marcus was a 26-year-old peacock who thought he was Morris Day. Besides his musical prowess, Marcus was known for being a mama's boy and washing his luxury cars daily while wearing a three-piece suit. But he was mad cool. And since I didn't hang out with anyone my age besides Rick, telling Marcus about my new relationship with April felt logical. So when he called me on Wednesday asking how things were going with me and Peaches, I sang like Luther Vandross. The last 72 hours had been a hotbed of activity, burning a hole in my teenage tongue. I needed to tell someone about my indoctrination into independent manhood. So Marcus' timing couldn't have been better.

After I told Marcus about April, he busted out laughing.

"Doc!! Are you talking about Mimi?" Marcus chortled,

"Who?" I said.

"Mimi. That's April's nickname."

"Hold up, bro! How do you know April?"

"Man, she and I went to junior college together. I know her whole family. Mimi's a good girl. But she's outta your league, Doc."

"Hold up! What do you mean outta my league? You think I'm too gully to pull someone like April?" I scoffed.

Marcus sighed. "Nah, Doc. Slow your roll. That's not what I'm saying. Shorty's too old for a young buck like you. Hell, she's too mature for me! Look, let me be real with you. Man to man. I know you feel like King Kong bagging an older chick. Kudos to you for that, by the way. But you're still in high school with lots more pussy to conquer. LOOOOTTTSSS! You feel me, Doc? You need to be out there sowing oats, not playing house. I know April. Mark my words, she'll break your heart."

I nodded at the receiver, thanked Marcus for the talk, and hung up. I knew he meant well, but Marcus didn't KNOW me. I knew what

I was doing. Hell, he was probably mad that April wouldn't give him any play and just wanted to be friends. This Morris Day wanna-be was about to find out, ain't nobody bad like ME.

Friday couldn't get here fast enough. I was busting at the seams because I could feel in my bones that it was gonna be *THE* night with April. And I had the perfect alibi to be out all night. I was going to a concert with Rick and Marcus at their church and then chilling afterward. So, Friday after school, I went home took a nap, worked out, showered, and had something to eat. Then I called my Mom at work to tell her I'd be hanging with Rick and Marcus for the night. She was cool with it. Everything was on lock.

The concert was BANGING!!! A guest community choir and some heavy hitter musicians rocked the rafters off the church. I was so caught up in the music, energy, and vibe that I'd lost track of time. The concert was still rocking at 9 pm, so I went downstairs to the church payphone and called April. She wasn't home, so I left a message. After the concert, I went to dinner with the band and singers and continued to call April. Still no answer. This went on until 11:30 pm when April finally answered. She'd been in time purgatory at the hair salon and was just getting home. She told me I was still welcome to come over if it wasn't too late. I assured her it wasn't too late and I'd be right over.

When I arrived at April's, she'd lit candles and set the mood. By the time I closed the door, said a silent prayer, and turned around, April was wearing nothing but a smile. It felt like a scene out of a movie. We went straight to the bedroom and literally went at it from midnight to 7 am the following day. April's freak flag had me reciting the pledge of allegiance while speaking in tongues. There was no end to the new experiences she took my body through. I was *whipped* and thoroughly baptized.

That morning, I was half asleep on April's lap while she spoke on the phone with her oldest sister, Danielle. April thought I was sound asleep, but I listened intently to their conversation. I guess I was the flavor of the week, and my age was a hot topic.

"But he's so young!" Danielle whooped.

April gushed, "I know he's young, but he's so mature. He works at the church and he drives his own car. And he's so nice."

Danielle sniffed "Yes, but he's still extremely young, Mimi. Nice or otherwise. I'm just saying to watch yourself. You know how you can get. Just promise you won't drag him too far, Mimi Mouse..."

I drifted back to sleep.

April's fluency in the male love languages of sex and food was on point. When I finally got up, she'd set out a breakfast spread fit for a lumberjack: grits, eggs, pancakes, fruit, bacon sausage, coffee, juice, YOU NAME IT! It was like I dreamed and woke up in heaven. I felt special, which was a first for me. If this was what playing outta my league felt like, I was content riding April's bench.

Despite all the communication that transpired between our bodies in the bedroom, April and I ate in silence. We exchanged a few awkward smiles and compliments on the food, but that was it. The gap between attraction and fulfillment had been filled. After breakfast, April told me she needed to get ready for work. I told her I needed to get home to prepare for rehearsal. We agreed to talk later in the day and went our separate ways. This would become the routine of our relationship.

## Gateway Drugs + Bitch Slaps

When it comes to faith and courage, everyone shares two common denominators – cussing and praying. Praying folks have faith; cussers convey courage. And those with the fortitude of both are a force to be reckoned with. I was a force. Not because my faith and courage co-conspired. No, my force stemmed from being a hopeless romantic with trust issues. But love without trust requires a strong agency over your personal space. When I was little, I claimed that space with shit, damn, motherfucker, and while I lay me down to sleep. But with the loss of innocence comes a theft of trust in yourself. So you need something stronger than cussing, praying, faith, and courage to mark your territory. For me, that was sex.

A week after our all-night romp, April and I finally confronted the elephant and 80-pound gorilla in the room: our ages. The "come to Jesus" talk about our budding May-December romance happened in our favorite place: the bed in April's apartment. I was basking in a post-coital contact high and apparently talking in my sleep. April jostled me awake, giggling.

"A nipple for your thoughts," she quipped.

"Huh?" I replied, dazed.

"You were talking in your sleep." She smirked.

"What was I saying? Do I need a lawyer? Please don't call my Mom!" I fake begged.

"There is no need for handcuffs... yet." She winked.

"You were talking gibberish and smiling... a lot. But I may need a lawyer if I call your Mom."

April's face turned to stone after the Mom comment. It wasn't a good look, and my body tensed.

"Hold up! Did I do something wrong?" I asked.

April grimaced and turned away from me. My heart dropped. I had no idea how to read the situation. What was happening? Several beats passed before April finally turned towards me again. I let out a huge gush of air, unaware I'd been holding my breath. April silently opened and closed her mouth to speak several times before looking at me. I stared back, nervous and clueless. I felt a drop of sweat trickle down my neck.

"I wanna ask you something, but I'm scared of your response." April finally spoke.

I scooted closer to her. She put her hand out to reestablish the distance. I calmly straightened my back. I needed to be an adult.

"You can ask me anything, April. I'm an open book." I held my breath again.

"How old are you?" April asked.

"I'm 17."

April's face turned ghostly. She cleared her throat and gave me a stern look. "Wait, how old are you? Her tone sounded like my Mom's.

"I'm 17," I repeated.

"SHITTTT!!!" she wheezed and rose from the bed.

"What's wrong? Did I do something wrong?" I asked again. She shook her head back and forth.

"I didn't think you were so young." her head dropped.

"Really? How old did you think I was? Wait, how old are YOU?" my eyebrow raised.

"I'm 25," she whispered.

"SHITTTT!!!" I roared. I didn't know if April wanted to hug me or burp me.

Before I went over that evening, I'd called April and asked her to be my girlfriend. I explained that I was extremely private and didn't trust folks from the outside. Growing up, it had been only me and my mom against the world, with no one else interfering in our relationship. I made it clear that now that I was an adult, I wanted the same thing with her. April agreed immediately and told me to get to her place ASAP to seal the deal. She confessed I was the best lover and now the best boyfriend she'd ever had.

April and I sat silently on opposite edges of her bed for about 20 minutes after the age reveal. The sound of our thought bubbles oscillating in the silence was deafening. I couldn't take it! I needed answers. NOW!!

I finally turned to April and barked, "Okay, are we still cool? Are you still my girlfriend?" It came out more like a command than a question.

She started to say something, then paused.

At this point, a thousand butterflies balled up in the pit of my stomach. And not the good kind. I knew this was it. April was gonna break up with me. It would go down as the shortest relationship in history.

But instead, she did the complete opposite. She explained she thought I was so much older because I drove my own car, had my own money, worked at the church, and came and went as I pleased. I couldn't reconcile this information in my brain. What she said made zero sense. Especially since Brenda was her sister. Brenda knew how old me and Rick were. So, April had to know, too. Right? But I didn't say a word.

April babbled on a bit more before announcing she liked what we had and wanted it to continue. I was SHOCKED. Our relationship would live to see another day. Despite all the doubts racing around in my head, my face and dick beamed their approval. This jailbait had officially taken the bait. I exhaled and took another hit of her pussy. I was hooked.

My new relationship with April was a literal fuck fest. It was me, April, and her bedsprings. Just how I wanted it. I thought I was the shit. Had a grown woman doing things to me that men twice my age only dreamed of. You couldn't tell me nothing! We were a month into the relationship, and I felt like Denzel Washington in *Training Day*. King Kong didn't have anything on me. But the Russians were coming, and my Aprilpalooza was about to get fucked up.

The first bomb came from another member of the Village People, Cedric Cox. Cedric was the church musical director, my boss, mentor, music teacher, father figure—pretty much a multi-hyphenate pain in my ass. He called and asked me to meet him on Thursday after school for a music lesson. I agreed and didn't think anything of it. Men's Day was coming up at the church, and I figured he wanted to start reviewing the songs we'd be performing. Of course, this wasn't the case. Cedric was usually waiting for me on the organ when I arrived. But today, there was a note on the organ bench asking me to come to his office. And if you knew Cedric, you'd understand why I immediately started checking myself for leaks. Cedric's vibe was a trinity of old Negro spirituals, sneaky uncles, and hard tests. And this meeting was the equivalent of being called to the principal's office without knowing what you did wrong. I crumpled up the note and silently swore under my breath. I was five minutes early. So, if I left now, I could lie and say I had to stay after school for band practice or detention. I picked up my backpack and made a beeline for the door. I was about to put my hand out to push it open when a voice said...

"Good day, Myles. It's always a blessing to see you here." It was Cedric's wife, Cynthia. She was the church secretary, and NOTHING slipped past her—not even me.

"Hi, Ms. Cynthia! I was just—"

"Cedric's waiting for you in his office." Cynthia interrupted. "He's anxious to speak with you. So you better head on down there. You know he doesn't like to be kept waiting." She put her hand on her hip as an exclamation point.

"Yes, ma'am!" I chirped. I knew if I even dreamt of saying something different to Ms. Cynthia, I'd have to wake up apologizing.

I trudged my way down the stairs to Cedric's torture chamber and knocked on the door. The door was cracked, so I slipped my head through the slit.

"Hey, Cedric. You wanted to talk to me?"

Cedric was sitting at his desk in a green, pleather, swivel recliner chair with his back turned to me. He turned the chair around to greet me like a scene out of *The Godfather*. Images of human sacrifices and ass whoopins flashed through my head. I gulped and stepped over the threshold, still checking for leaks.

"Sit down, Myles," Cedric said abruptly. He and Cynthia never called me Mylo. They believed in formalities and whatnot. I sat my sweaty ass down.

"Are you and that Barnes girl having relations?" Cedric asked, stone-faced.

I flinched.

"Oh! We're going concrete dick, no Vaseline, I see." I sensed this was man talk, so I set the tone and leaned forward.

"Who told you that?" I asked.

Cedric leaned back and folded his arms over his chest.

"The Barnes were almost my in-laws, you know," Cedric revealed.

"Danielle and I were hot and heavy back in the day. Dated for five years. We even got engaged. But that's a story for another day. Anyway, we still talk, and she called me the other day to tell me you and April are fucking. Is it true?" Cedric's face was still stony.

"Yes, me and April are an item," I responded.

"I didn't ask about *items*. This conversation isn't about a damn grocery store, Myles. I asked if the two of you are fucking. Having relations. Knocking boots, like you young cats like to say. So what's the story, Myles?" Cedric's face was balled up like a fist. I sat in disbelief for a few seconds before responding.

"Yes, we're fucking. But she's also my girlfriend. We've been together a month." I shut up before I dug a deeper hole for myself. I didn't know how much he knew.

Cedric stared past me, emotionless. He positioned his elbows on top of the desk and lowered his glasses.

"BE. VERY. CAREFUL." Cedric's words were calm. His tone made me shiver.

"You come across more grown than you are, Myles. Ray Charles can see that. But you're still a little piss ant. You wear that old soul of yours on your sleeve. It's a blessing and a curse, Myles." Cedric's pitch sharpened. "Your level of maturity can open doors and keep you trapped. You hear what I'm saying, Myles? You're loyal with a heart to match. But with a woman April's age, you gotta be careful. She'll easily take advantage of your youth. Trap your black ass in a revolving door of hurt."

Cedric pushed his glasses back up the bridge of his nose and stood up. I took the cue and stood up, too.

"But worse, Myles, she WILL break your heart. I promise you that! She'll break your heart, Myles. Mark my words. But you'll be okay. That crotchety old soul of yours will be your resilience. So have your fun with that older coochie. Get your kicks and giggles. But leave it there.

You hear me? *Do* you hear me, Myles?" Cedric glared at me over the top of his glasses.

"Hit it and quit it. There's more to life than being grown. Don't EVER forget that." Cedric patted me on the shoulder and walked out. He didn't summon me to follow him.

I hadn't spoken to Peaches since she'd left skid marks in our driveway. So when she called me out of the blue the day after my talk with Cedric, I was shocked. There was no hello, what's up, how's it hanging... Peaches just dove in screaming. She'd heard that I was in a relationship with an older woman.

I was like, "Who told you that?"

She told me not to worry about it and asked again if it was true.

I said yes, it was.

Peaches started yelling again so loud and fast; I swear dogs started lining up outside our door.

She finally calmed down, and I asked if she was finished.

She quietly said yes. Then Peaches hit me with those cold ass words again, "You'll never find anybody better than me, EVER!"

I sighed, asked if her back hurt from kissing her own ass, then hung up on her. The dig felt good.

Peaches called right back and started telling me off some more.

I told her to go fuck herself three times 'til Tuesday and hung up again.

She called right back.

This time, I hung the phone up without answering it.

This went on four more times. I finally picked up the receiver and left it off the ringer. I'd had enough. She could yell at the busy signal all she wanted. But Peaches was far from finished with me...

I'd made it through the weekend without another sneak attack. But Monday was a brutal bitch. Rick was avoiding me. I got a C- on my trigonometry test, and when I went to my car during 7th-period study hall, there was a note under my windshield wiper with "*IT'S. NOT. OVER.*" scrawled in Peaches' handwriting. *Manic Monday* played on the car radio during the drive home from school. Millie Jackson was playing when I got inside the house. This meant Mom was home early from work. It also meant I couldn't watch the porno my boy Candy Man had lent me for the evening. Monday had cock blocked, and bitch slapped me. I told you: brutal bitch.

Mom was on the phone with one of her girls. "Yeah girl, let me get back to Millie. She getting funky with the cats and dogs." Listening to R&B music made my Mom think she was smooth. It reminded me of the fun and laughter she and my dad used to have when they weren't in church mode. She saw me enter the room and held up her finger for me to wait. Mom put down the receiver and asked me to get her a glass of Pepsi with extra ice. I reminded her it was bad for her diabetes. Mom reminded me she could slap me into next week if I needed my check early. I sniggled and got her drink.

"If YOU pour it, I'm not responsible." I put the soda can and glass of ice in front of her and winked. Mom pointed to the album on the table. It was the *Back to the Sh**t* cover with Millie Jackson sitting on a toilet with her panties around her ankles.

"So, who's been sitting on your toilet, Junior?" Mom opened the can of Pepsi, poured it into the glass, and then took a sip like she'd just asked me how my day went.

My face must have registered 50 shades of stupid because that's how I felt. If I had been the one drinking the Pepsi, I would have sprayed my Mom with it in response. "Well, hello to you too, Mom. How was your day?" I was attempting to avoid her verbal jab.

"Sit. We need to catch up." Mom motioned to the dining room chair next to her and patted the seat. I obeyed the request, trying not to resist for too long. Mom only called me Junior when she was fishing for info. She was the original Gossip Girl.

"What's Millie got you thinking about, Mom? You got dirt to dish?"

I was still dodging. The way my day was going, Daphne Gunn was the land mine ready to detonate what was left of my shitty day. Mom took an ice cube from the top of her glass and popped it in her mouth. The intro to Millie's *Love Stinks* monolog started playing in the background. Tick...tick...

"How are things with you and Peaches?" BOOM! There it was. Fire in the hole.

"She still sitting on your toilet seat or has she found a new stall?"

Mom took another drag from her glass. She may have left work early but was still on the job.

"You asking or confirming?" I'd finally found my voice.

Mom just sat there, staring.

I caved. "Peaches and I broke up. There! Are you and Millie happy now? Love stinks!" I grumbled and averted my gaze.

Mom put her hand on my forearm and gently squeezed it.

"I'm sorry to hear that Mylo. Are you okay? You wanna talk about it?" Mom's tone was sincere. She'd blown up my spot and patched it in one fell swoop.

"No, I'm cool." I looked at her again.

"It was a long time coming and needed to happen. Peaches wasn't good for me. I realize that now. But going back to your tacky toilet metaphor, I'm the one who's found the new stall. Not Peaches." I responded.

Mom stopped mid-sip. "Oh really? Is there a name on this stall I should know about?"

"Her name is April, Mom. She's beautiful and treats me like a king. Not like the Joker Peaches tried to make me into with all her foolishness." I sneered.

My mom's expression remained neutral.

"Mom, I want you to meet April. Can I invite her to family dinner this week?" Family dinner occurred every Saturday at my mom's best friend Ava's house. Both were single moms (Ava had five kids), so we shared weekend meals.

Mom squeezed my arm again. "Sure. I'd love to meet April. I'll tell Ava to add another plate for Saturday." We both smiled.

"And thank you for telling me, Mylo. Just promise me you'll be nice to Peaches. She still loves you. And although you feel disrespected, you don't want to hurt her any more than you already have. Okay?"

I nodded. Mom stood up and kissed the top of my head. I sat for a moment, still shell-shocked. My Mom had already known.

I needed a reprieve from Millie's toilet talk, so I went to my bedroom. My first order of business was to call April and invite her to family dinner. She happily accepted and invited me to her parents' house for dinner the following weekend. My next call was to Rick's house. He'd been dodging me like a sweaty jock strap all weekend, and I couldn't figure out why. We told each other EVERYTHING. So his ducking and diving had me on high alert.

Once I got Rick on the phone, he sang like Freddie Jackson. I barely said hello before he started confessing and apologizing. Peaches had visited him to interrogate him about my situation. She'd somehow found out about him sneaking around with Brenda and threatened to tell his parents if he didn't spill the beans. Rick told Peaches EVERYTHING, then agreed to put her shady note on my windshield for extra insurance. I couldn't believe my best friend had dimed me ALL the way out!!! I was in such disbelief I couldn't even bring myself to respond. I just hung up the phone and took it off the hook so Rick couldn't call back. I'd been bitch slapped enough for one day. King Kong could have this one.

Rick and I avoided each other the rest of the week. His shame and my temper both needed time to cool. Besides, I had bigger fish to fry: the family dinner with April and my Mom. I hadn't told my Mom about April's age. I figured that was better revealed in public to prevent me and/or April from a hospital visit at my mother's hands. So, that was the bullet I focused on dodging the remainder of the week. Something told me I would need ALL my strength and faculties for this one.

My mom made my favorite meal for the family dinner with April – spaghetti and meatballs. It was a crowd-pleaser capable of feeding six greedy teenagers with room for leftovers. April's introduction to my Mom, however, wasn't so palatable. Our family dinners normally buzzed with tons of chatter, laughter, and warmth. Today's dinner served up lots of icy glares and saccharine politeness. The tipping point was when my Mom saw April rubbing my inner thigh under the table. Ava caught wind of the sighting and quietly kept my Mom from lunging across the table. April swiftly took her hand away from my thigh. But not before Ava's 12-year-old daughter (who had an enormous crush on me) conveniently dropped her meatball on April's lap while angling for seconds. We never made it to dessert.

While first impressions may have been DOA at dinner, my mother's brilliance as a youth counselor reigned supreme that night. Mom made me ride with her to Ava's house, knowing it would be a

45-minute drive both ways. So what we lacked in table banter was about to be made up for on the drive home. We were on the road about 10 minutes when my mom started singing...

*On top of spaghetti,*
*All covered with crap.*
*Desiree dropped a meatball.*
*On poor April's lap.*

I gave my Mom a side eye and said, "You're serving corn with your spaghetti now, I see."

"Yep, they call me Chef Cornardee. You better recognize!" my Mom retorted.

We both giggled.

"Mom, I really like April and could see myself with her forever. I..."

"Stop right there," my mom interjected.

"You don't have to justify your decisions to me. You're grown. So if you're looking for me to wag my finger or shame you, you're gonna be disappointed." She put her blinker on to turn.

"Mylo, I trust you. I love you. And most of all, I respect you. My love for you as a mother is unconditional. My love for you is also independent of the choices you make. I want you to own your happiness and your mistakes. And know that the right people will love you despite either. Remember that."

Mom kept her eyes focused while we drove a few more miles in silence.

"Mylo, promise me you'll be careful. I'm not talking about sex. I'm talking about your heart. I didn't say anything before, but I don't approve of your age gap or the fact you tried to sugarcoat it with this family dinner." She turned to see the surprised look on my face.

"Yeah, son. You ain't slick!" she teased.

"But seriously, BE CAREFUL. You're dealing with real grown folks' business now. And although you're mature for your age, this is more responsibility than you're used to. I'm not saying you can't handle it. I'm simply asking you to proceed with caution. And know that I'm ALWAYS here if you EVER need to talk about ANYTHING. I'm here for you no matter what."

I laid my head on Mom's arm as she turned the car onto our driveway. She turned off the ignition and hugged me tight. It was the safest I'd ever felt.

*Guess Who's Coming to Dinner* Part Two with April's family was a polar opposite experience. Meeting April's parents was like meeting Diahann Carroll and Melvin Van Peebles as a couple. They looked and acted like the Black bourgeoisie. I'd already met April's mom since she was in the church Sanctuary Choir and loved to watch me play the organ and piano. Colette Barnes had a prickly personality with a face that wore a smile and a frown at the same time – like a sly fox. I'd learn later how sly she was. April's father, Todd Barnes, was as handsome as he was cool. He had an athletic build and could probably steal your woman without blinking.

The people, food, and music flowed abundantly, and everybody appeared not to have a care in the world. Coming from a home where it was just me and my mom, experiencing this was a culture shock. I wasn't used to having people coming and going at any given time. I grew up respecting home as a place of peace and personal space. But the Barnes' home was intentionally crafted without boundaries. It was a space where anything was game.

Mr. and Mrs. Barnes accepted me with open arms and were okay with April and my age gap. I was welcomed into their home and treated like their son. Mr. Barnes even set up an electric piano at their house so I could rehearse for church and entertain their guests. They made space for me and gave me a sense of belonging without rules or limitations. That's no disrespect to my Mom. She gave me freedom, respect and treated me like an adult. But with Barnes, well, it was at the next level. In the beginning, it felt like a party every time I visited them. Little did I know, it was all a setup.

April and her family treated me like royalty. It was a stark contrast to the servant I'd been to Peaches' chaos. It felt like a much-needed change for me. The Barnes gave me a sense of purpose as April's boyfriend and granted me entrance into their carefully curated circle. So, with my newfound identity as the Fresh Prince of the Barnes, April's family became my new community, using their charms and influence to save me from my world of insecurities.

But had I known all that ego-stroking was merely grooming me for a bigger world of pain, I would have stayed my ass at home.

*******************************************************************************

JODY PASCHAL

# Collective Bargaining

## Burning Bridges and Taking Names

# Tugether

Like it or not, we're all systemically programmed to dislike ourselves. It's the cornerstone of capitalism and economics. The commoditization of insecurity, fear, and the reality that happiness is a moving target. But sometimes you need to burn a bridge to keep from crossing it again. And 2020 was that bridge. You see, the true meaning of liberation is belonging everywhere and nowhere at once. So, in a sense, the global pandemic gave us a collective moment of liberation. It was a forced metamorphosis we weren't prepared for or knew that we needed. It isolated us, stripped us down, and forced us to face all our ugly bits so we could appreciate our REAL selves—flaws and all.

A person needs a reason to get out of bed in the morning. But life can hock a huge loogie in your face even after you find it. And right now, COVID was the ocean of all loogies. Before the pandemic, the one thing I looked forward to most was going to the gym. The release of sweat, endorphins, smack talk, and fat cells was my happy place and coping mechanism.

But Corona had closed all the gyms and parks. So, when the dumbbells and *Beach Body* videos in my basement had run their course, I decided to take on nature. I was like the mailman—no matter rain, snow, sleet, or hail, I was delivering the pain to silence my thoughts. I started working out at a high school football field near my house and met a group of guys there that changed my life.

It was the butt crack of dawn the Tuesday before my 50$^{th}$ birthday. I was running down the stadium stairs when a group of six guys carrying cinder blocks jogged through the entrance. They looked haggard, like they'd just returned from war. They went onto the field and began doing some CrossFit exercises with the cinder blocks. Later, they took out a frisbee and started throwing it up and down the field for the group to catch. If someone missed a catch, the group had to stop and do an exercise.

I watched them briefly, then suddenly heard, "Heads up!" The frisbee was flying straight towards my head.

But instead of catching it, I ducked. When I stood up, one of the guys was yelling at me. "That'll cost you 10 burpees! Start on my count!"

I looked around to see who he was talking to.

"Dude, I'm talking to you. You missed the catch, so now you've gotta pay in burpees. Come on! On my count! Down, one!"

I fell in line without question.

Once we finished the burpee set, all six of the men came over to greet me. They explained that they were from the neighborhood and saw one another exercising on the field when the pandemic hit, so they decided to work out as a group. They met Tuesdays, Thursdays, and Saturdays, and after Saturday workouts, they'd get coffee to shoot the shit. They invited me to be the lucky number seven in their makeshift group.

"Sure, I'd love to join you guys! Thanks for including me. By the way, my name is—"

Before I could finish, the guy who seemed like the head honcho interrupted me. "Hold up there, buddy. We don't use our names in this group. We assign you an alias based on your backstory." The head honcho sounded like a military brass.

"Think of it like an AA meeting. But instead of booze, we focus on fitness. You leave it all on the field. Vegas rules and whatnot. So let's assign your alias, and then we'll tell you ours. Don't want you mucking up our creative process." The honcho gave me a salute, and I returned the favor."Oh, are you military, Mr. Ultimate Frisbee?"

"Former military. I served in the Air Force in the 90s. You military, too?" I responded.

"Yep, I'm still on active duty. Army JAG, 28 years," the honcho beamed. "But enough about me. We need to get you a name so I can get to work. Where ya from, and what do you do when you're not ducking frisbees?" the honcho inquired.

"I'm originally from Buffalo, NY but have lived in the DC area with my wife for almost 15 years. No kids, in case you're wondering. My wife couldn't handle another me in the house."

That earned me a few chuckles and some head nods.

"I work as a facilities manager for a government contractor. So I have to get to work, too." I said.

The guys nodded their approval, huddled, and whispered like kids strategizing a kickball game. Every few seconds, a guy glanced my way as if he were studying a science project. After about a minute, they walked towards me. The youngest looking guy in the group drew the short straw to give me my new name.

"Okay. Although you suck at frisbee, based on the way you hauled ass on those stairs over there, you have the need for speed. So that being said, we hereby name you..." e put his finger up. "Wait for it..."

The guys pounded their hands against their legs for a drum roll.

"TOP GUN! Don't let your ego write checks your body can't cash."

The young dude and the rest of the crew clapped and took turns fist-bumping me.

Then honcho took over. "Okay, moving along. Now it's time for you to meet the crew." honcho declared. "They call me Nut Job because I have two ex-wives and a current wife on the brink who are all bat shit crazy. The whippersnapper who told you your name, that's Audio. He's always got his earbuds on. This guy over here is Pac-Man. He still holds the high score at his hometown arcade. The dude with the headband over there is Dugout. He coaches a little league baseball team that catches about as well as you do. Fancy pants over there with the neon shorts is Karaoke. Don't EVER ask him to sing. And last, we have Bones. He's also from Buffalo and produces one of those crazy true crime podcasts my wife can't get enough of. I'm still convinced we should have named him Oprah."

I could tell the smack talk in this group would be epic.

This whole crew would have been shift managers on the Island of Misfit Toys. Each of them had an alias and a dysfunction that needed an alpha male support group. And my busted behind fit right into their reindeer games. I'd found my tribe and inadvertently given the group its name.

The Misfits kicked my ass on the field for the next week and twice on Saturday. I'd slipped up and told the guys it was my 50th birthday. But instead of high-fives and cupcakes, I got my face cracked.

"Good work, you minions!" Dugout was leading today's session. "You know what time it is. Top Gun, get your old ass over here and close us out so I can get my caffeine fix."

The Misfits had a little closing ritual after each workout. They worked that whole AA meeting angle by selecting a guy to share something encouraging or relevant before we jumped ship. So, since I was the birthday boy, it was my turn to be indoctrinated.

"Okay, you rotten bastards. Since it's MY day, I'm making an executive decision to change up the vibe in this bitch. Everybody social distance in a circle and put your hand in like this." I got a few eye rolls and "ahh fucks," then everyone was in position.

"Now, on the count of three, shout 'tugether' and break."

The whole group froze and looked at me like I'd stepped in shit.

"Say what now?" Pac-Man questioned.

"Hahaha! Now I've got your attention. Say 'TUGETHER.'" I looked around and paused for dramatic effect. "Okay, here's the deal. I had a speech impediment as a kid, and until the 6th grade thought the word together was pronounced 'tugether'. So now when I work out, I say tugether to remind myself how far I've come. Not too shabby for a 50-year-old muscle head, if I must say so myself."

I brushed my shoulders and did The Dougie dance to showboat. More eye rolls and cussing followed.

"So again, on the count of three, everyone shout, TUGETHER! One...Two..."

Before I got to three, everyone mumbled 'break' and flipped me the bird as they walked to their cars.

"Save that Dance Fever shit for your wife, Magic Mike!" Karaoke bellowed.

Dugout turned around, grabbed his crotch, and yelled, "I've got your TUGether right here, Top Gun!"

Oh, and the little shits made me pay for everyone's coffee. Who said membership has its benefits? Happy motherfucking birthday to me.

The weekly workouts became my new religion. I was drinking the Gatorade; praising the holy trinity of trash talk, squats, and Icy Hot. Most importantly, I learned lessons in humility from a bunch of heathens. Having a sense of community outside of work and home felt good. I loved the Misfits like a cold sore. Because, let's face it, guys are assholes. But they were getting me out of the house, away from my thoughts and back in my slim fits. There was glory in the gloom.

The darkness before dawn provided me with a sense of peace every Tuesday, Thursday, and Saturday. It gave me something to look forward to, restored some agency over my life, and made me feel like myself. Yes, things were finally starting to look up for your boy, Mylo. *Then. Shit. Got. Real.*

The honeymoon ended two months after I joined the Misfits. I was getting ready for our Thursday morning beatdown and turned on my phone. The rapid-fire text notifications that followed sounded like a pinball machine. At first, I thought they were building alerts from work. But Bones had sent out a group text, and the responses were coming in hot. Turns out Pac-Man and Nut Job tested positive for COVID. So for safety's sake, the Misfits paused workouts for a few weeks. It felt like two steps forward and ten steps back. I'm surprised there were any survivors from all the f-bombs I dropped. It was a bitter pill, but we choked it down and made lemon wedges out of the situation.

We tried doing workouts together on Zoom, but it was a hot ass mess. Lunges hit differently when delivered with a side of butt crack theater on a 27-inch monitor. So we decided to table group workouts until our self-imposed quarantine was over. Until then, the only glue holding us together was a Misfit Slack channel Audio started to keep the shit show in motion. It was the epicenter of extra that was always stirring up shit or stepping in it. And on this particular day, it was both.

They say people are more truthful early in the morning or when physically tired. The body's at rest, the mind's at ease, and thoughts and emotions are clear. So, in a sense, morning workouts are a natural truth serum. The balance of darkness, quiet, and shared experience creates a vulnerability that lets you know folks on a different level. Well, today, I learned that a pandemic, too much testosterone, and a social media channel produce a similar kind of vulnerability—but on steroids.

The conversation started innocently around 7 am. I was getting ready for work, and Karaoke was getting dragged on Slack for posting pics of some ugly new workout gear he'd purchased.

**#themisfits**

**Bones**

*Karaoke, I swear those colors aren't found anywhere in nature. WTH!?!?!*

**Top Gun**

*That outfit needs orange cones and police tape around it 'cause it's a damn crime scene!*

**Pac Man**

*Did you let your three-year-old pick that shit out for you? Wait, are those dinosaur laces?*

**Dugout**

*Yeah, man. You should have embossed Tootie Fruity My Booty across it.*

**Nut Job**

*What do you know about fruity booties, Dugout? Is there something you're not telling us???*

**Dugout**

*Don't worry Nut Job. You're not my type. You've got too much ex-factor. I like 'em young and tender like Audio.* 😉

**Audio**

*@Dugout You need to stop before I turn your ass into a MeToo hashtag.*

**Dugout**

*@Audio Don't bitch up on me, sugar tits. Save that #MeToo nonsense for your girlfriend.*

**Top Gun**

*What you saying, Dugout? You think #MeToo only applies to women?*

**Dugout**

*@Top Gun Sound it out, Gloria Steinem.*

**Top Gun**

*@Dugout Hooked on phonics worked for me, Fred Flintstone. But tell me, is yabba dabba doo code for misogynist?*

**Dugout**

*What's your deal? Did some chick make you blush, and have you crying in your milk? I never took you for a punk ass, Top Gun.*

**Top Gun**

*@Dugout It's a shame assholes can't smell themselves. For your information, I was 12 years a slave in my 1st marriage to a Mrs. Robinson, who groomed me at 17 to be her caretaker. So #MeToo motherfucker!*

**Dugout**

*@Top Gun I'm sorry, man. I didn't know. Seriously, I didn't mean anything by it. You know how we joke around. I didn't mean what I said. Honestly.*

The chat went silent. I took a few deep breaths and then shut off my phone. I wasn't in the mood for questions. Besides, I needed to get to work.

I headed to the football field after work to blow off some steam. I'd let my emotions get the best of me; it wasn't a good look. Petra called me the Grinch who stole Tuesday. She wasn't wrong. I'd reacted like my heart was two sizes too small. And if Dugout knew I was comparing him to Suzie Who, he'd beat me like I stole something. I wasn't proud of my behavior and wasn't ready to face the music either. So, for now, I'd work it out on the field.

I did a few warmup exercises to get in the spirit, then ran around the track. The cadence on the pavement calmed my mind. *You should never put yourself in a position to apologize*. I let the mantra fuel my pace.

I was hitting my stride when I heard someone yell, "Watch your form!" It was Bones. I slowed my pace and put my elbows on my knees to catch my breath.

Bones walked towards me. "Great minds think alike, I see. I came out here to clear my head, too." He sat his gym bag on the grass.

I nodded to him in agreement, still winded.

"Sooooo... What happened this morning? You okay? I mean, I know you're not a morning person and all, but DAMN!!"

Bones comment made me grin a bit. "I know. When it comes to me and mornings, my wife says you have to tap lightly like a woodpecker with a headache." I joked.

Bones broke out laughing. "I need to meet your wife. She sounds kinder and gentler than your first one."

I gave Bones a sideways glance. "You trying to Dr. Phil me right now?" I asked.

"Nah, I'm Woody Woodpecker. Want some Advil?" Bones and I laughed and gave each other a dap.

"Man, I don't know what happened. Dugout... I mean... I guess I..."

"Don't sweat it, dawg. You're allergic to assholes, and Dugout made you sneeze. I get it. But that's not what I'm talking about. There's something else going on besides shit-scented pollen. You wanna talk about it?" Bones offer sounded sincere, and I was fresh out of fucks.

"Yeah, I guess I need to talk to something other than the paper," I confessed.

Bones gave me a quizzical look.

"Since the pandemic and my 50th, I've been wrestling with chandelier moments from my past, and it's fucking with my head. So my co-worker suggested I write everything down to keep from going postal. But based on this morning's drama, that's not cutting it. So tag, you're it." I stared at the pavement.

"I've got you, dawg. Remember, I listen to people for a living. And we've got that Misfit, Vegas rules, AA meeting pledge thing we're bound to. So give it to me straight, no chaser. I can handle whatever you throw at me." Bones put his hand on my shoulder. I broke down.

For the next 10 minutes, I spilled the tea, coffee, and brown liquor about my groomed epiphany at the office. Bones listened calmly and intently—never interrupting or passing judgment—not even during the E.T. references on Planet of the Aints. It reminded me of the talks I used to have with my mom. I felt my jaw relax.

"Hey, buddy. You still gettin' a workout in?" I asked.

"Yeah, that's still the plan. You joining me?" Bones responded.

"Nope. But I'll be right back. Don't leave!" I jogged the distance to my car and got in. I knew what I had to do.

Bones was stretching near the fence when I returned. His shirt was drenched in sweat, so I knew he'd done some damage.

"You leave it on the field?" I yelled.

"Yep. Yours too. I'm generous like that. Whatcha got behind your back?" Bones inquired.

"Here." I held out my journal. "This is me talking to the paper. It's just the beginning, but I think you'll get the gist. I trust you."

Bones looked at the journal, then me, and back to the journal. "Why do you want me to read this? You don't know me from a can of paint." Bones questioned.

"Like you said, you listen to people's crimes for a living. Maybe you can help with mine." I said earnestly.

"Fair enough." Bones smiled, then took the journal from me and placed it in his bag. "I'll read it tonight. Then we can arrange a time for me to return it. Sounds like you're not done with it yet."

"That's where I'm hoping you'll help." I held my fist out for a final dap, and we went our separate ways. One down, one to go...

Now that I'd made amends with Bones, I needed to face the rest of the Misfits. But I'd already been called a punk once and didn't want to co-sign that with a weak-ass apology. I had to bring my A-game. You know what they say: a stiff apology is a second insult.

So, I decided to return to the scene of the crime. I turned on my phone, scrolled to the Slack app, and opened the Misfit group chat. My first post was a GIF of Ricky Ricardo and Lucille Ball with the caption *'Lucy! You Got Some Splainin' to Do!'* My next post was a pic that read, *'I try to save my apologies for what I've done later in the week.'* Finally, I posted a GIF of Don Cheadle that read, 'Oh man, *I'm sorry bout that.'* Then I sat back and waited.

Within five minutes, I got likes from Audio, Karaoke, Pac Man, and Bones. Nut Job commented 15 minutes later with 'ALL GOOD' and a salute emoji. There was radio silence from Dugout. I put my phone down and went to the kitchen. My wife Traci was at the sink washing dishes. I walked up behind her and playfully swatted her buttocks. Traci dipped her hand in the dishwater, flicked some in my face, and handed me a towel. She washed while I dried and told her about the text apology to the Misfits and giving my journal to Bones. Afterward, Traci smiled, tapped a cloud of bubbles on the tip of my nose, and told me how proud she was of me. I blushed like a five-year-old while we finished the dishes.

An hour later, I checked my phone. Still nothing from Dugout. He was as stubborn as the eight-year-olds he coached. I was about to crawl into bed when my phone notification went off. I slid my phone off the nightstand and turned it over. I had a DM on Slack. It was Dugout.

*"Hey, Top Gun. I'm not being petty. I just didn't want to fuck around and say the wrong thing – AGAIN. I tend to milk things too much and then dislike what I spit up. I'm REALLY sorry for triggering you this morning. It was insensitive of me. But seriously, I'm all bark and no bite. This pandemic has made me a sad sack of ass, and I can't seem to turn it off. It doesn't give me the right to take it out on you guys, though. Man, I appreciate you! Even if my words and home training don't reflect it. So if you ever need to talk, I'm here for you, bro. We gotta hold each other up. It's hard out here for a pimp. 😉"*

I responded with a heart emoji and a thumbs-up emoji. A few seconds later, Dugout liked my Don Cheadle post. It was the hakuna matata moment I'd been waiting for. Order had been restored. I smiled and turned off the light.

Bones texted me a few days later and asked me to meet him for a beer after work to return my journal. He mentioned the place had outdoor seating and that our conversation needed something stronger than coffee. I wasn't sure what that meant. A conversation requiring liquid courage was never a good sign. But I texted back a thumbs up and let my wife know it would be every man for himself for dinner.

I pulled up to the restaurant around 5:15 pm. Only a handful of people were there, so I immediately spotted Bones. He'd snagged us a table outside and was already sipping a beer.

I pulled up a chair and ordered the specialty brew on tap when the server came around. I was as nervous as a hooker in church. I had no idea what Bones may or may not say. I'd put myself ALL THE WAY out there with him and wasn't sure I was ready for the fallout.

The server sat my beer down in front of me a few minutes later, and I took a huge gulp. I finally understood the need for the liquid courage.

"Dawg, why are you looking at me like your dad after a long day? No one's putting you on punishment," Bones said. "Exhale and enjoy your beer. I promise I come in peace. Here."

Bones placed my journal on the table. There were a bunch of blue sticky notes jutting out of it. "Thank you again for trusting me with this. I know it wasn't easy for you." He took another sip from his beer.

"What's with all the sticky notes? You tagging evidence or something?" I puckered my brows and folded my arms to imitate a detective.

"You look like you should be stroking a white cat while twirling a handlebar mustache. But no, Snidely Whiplash, the sticky notes aren't clues. They're reference markers. But let's not get ahead of ourselves. I've got a proposition for you."

I scowled at him and lowered my glass.

"What do you mean by proposition? I'm paying for my own drinks, and my wife can kick your ass. So don't get any funny ideas. I have standards ya know."

"Ladies and gentlemen, please welcome Top Gun to the party! I was beginning to wonder if you'd show up" Bones roared.

"You know I've gotta give the people what they want. I'm a one-man party bus." I smirked.

Bones rolled his eyes and opened up the journal. "On a serious note. THIS right here is powerful." He double-tapped the words on the page. "I know what you've written so far is just the beginning, but WHEW!" He thumbed through the pages as he spoke. "I've only known you 10 minutes, but it's incredible that you went through this and ended up the person you are. I have a whole new respect for you, Top Gun. That's the truth."

"Thank you, man. I needed to hear that. I'm still wrapping my brain around the realization myself. Turning 50 has given me a new perspective. I'm seeing my life with a completely different prescription in my lens, and it's a serious head fuck."

I tapped my knife on the table. I felt exposed.

"Well, I feel honored to be trusted with your story, Top Gun. Which brings me to my proposition." Bones repositioned himself in his chair. You could tell he was going into business mode.

"As you know, I work as a producer for a true crime podcast. Part of my job is developing ideas and topics for the show. And I'd like to pitch your story for an upcoming episode."

Bones folded his hands and leaned forward on the table.

Astonished, I sat with my mouth wide open."Shit. Are you serious?" I ran my hand over the top of my head. "You think MY story is interesting enough to be on a podcast? Wait, don't these stories have to be about crime and folks making bones into windchimes or something crazy like that?" I was seriously dazed and confused.

Bones chuckled at my response. "So, hear me out. Our broadcast company wants to ride the momentum of the #MeToo movement and give it a fresh voice. Because, at the end of the day, sexual and emotional abuse *are* true crimes. The carnage just looks different. And so far, the narrative has only been about men abusing women. But men *are* victims, too. And not just at the hands of other men. The Mrs. Robinson's of the world have their fair share of body counts, too. After reading your journal, I think your story is a unique example that sheds light on the issue. So, what do you think?"Bones leaned back in his seat and relaxed his shoulders.

My mouth was still agape. "Well, damn. I may need another beer to process all of this."

I put my elbow on the table and rested my forehead in my palm. Clearly, the Planet of the Aints wasn't done with me yet. I sat in silence for a few minutes. This was surreal, and I felt a bit overwhelmed.

Bones didn't press and gave me space to calm down. He continued to sip his beer and took out his phone to show me pics of his niece. She was nine months old with an adorable face that could diffuse any situation. But I could tell Bones was running out of baby anecdotes, and the server had brought me another beer.

So, I reentered the conversation. "Okay, Bones, tell me more about this proposal. What do you need me to do?"

"All right then. So first, I need to sell the idea to the broadcast brass since the concept is slightly different from the initial angle we were gunning for. Once I get the green light, we begin crafting the story. This is where you and the blue sticky notes come in. I'll give you some journal prompts to help shape the story's direction. If you're up for it, I can text you the first prompts tonight so you can start working on them. No pressure; you can take whatever time and space you need to answer the prompts. I want you to feel comfortable. Sound like a good plan to you so far?"

"WOW! I don't know what to say. I'm flabbergasted." I paused for several beats. "Fuck it! Hell yeah, I'm in! Send me the prompts. Mold me, Yoda. Take me to your leader. Go forth and prosper. Bring on all that shit!" I was tired of fighting with my thoughts.

We toasted to the decision and ordered some Buffalo wings while Bones walked me through the sticky notes. In my mind, all I could hear was, "Buckle up!".

*******************************************************************************

# PART 2
# Growing Pains

# Growth Spurt

Growth spurts are nothing more than seasonal changes in human form. We all cycle through maturation points—winters, springs, summers, falls—seasons where everything changes. You wake up one morning and appear to have physically and emotionally grown five inches. It's an empowering, beautiful stew of possibilities. The will it, won't it of it all. You've outgrown the people and things around you, only to realize you exist in unchartered territory. It's a strange purgatory of thought, emotion, and reality. But in the absence of belonging, there's always pain.

The months leading up to my coming of age were mildly eventful. By the grace of God (and my Mom's coercion), I graduated high school. Rick was dating Peaches now, and, for obvious reasons, we didn't talk much.

April and I had been on again and off again for eight months, and the seesaw ride had kept me in bed. When April and I were together, we romped in her sheets. When we broke up, I sulked in mine. I'd developed a social atrophy and identity crisis I hadn't imagined for myself at 18. Collateral damage from being an old soul, I suppose. April would break up with me in search of bigger fish to fry. And when she ran out of fish grease, my gullible ass was waiting in the wings for her holding a Filet-O-Fish sandwich. I was depressed and confused.

The world was supposed to be my oyster. But instead, the oyster and the ever-looming question of what's next were giving me serious stank eye. I was officially a grown-ass man with no plan. I felt small. And for the first time in my life, immature.

Incidentally, the weekend of my 18th birthday was a precursor to things to come. My teenage years had already been a soap opera of sexcapades, cheating, lies, and run-ins with my mother's belt. But nothing prepared me for the dramatic cast change I was about to have from *The Young and the Chestless* to *General Hospital.* Everything up until this point was merely a commercial break.

While growing up, celebrating birthdays had never been a big deal for me. I'd never had a birthday party, or much fuss made about me growing into myself. A few practical gifts, some wise words, and my Mom's famous coconut lemon cake—that was the extent of the fanfare. Truth be told, getting older was about as eventful as taking out the trash. It was a dirty obligation people only paid attention to when it stunk. But turning 18 was a HUGE deal. And I wanted my 18th birthday to stink to the high heavens.

Luckily, the birthday plans came to me. First, my Dad called and asked me to drop by his apartment for lunch. I was surprised since he rarely spent special occasions with me. But I appreciated the invitation and looked forward to seeing him. Despite my resentment, I still wanted my Dad to notice me. When I arrived at Dad's place, two of his work buddies were chilling in the living room watching *The Price is Right*. They were in a heated argument over the value of a baker's rack and waved past me when I walked in. I named them Heckle and Jeckle.

I noticed a TV tray set up in front of Dad's good recliner with three hoagies, curly fries, and a gallon of pineapple soda waiting to be dealt with. Dad knew food was my happy place and had all my favorites lined up. He was in the kitchen fiddling with an ice tray and gave me the nod, signaling it was okay to get my grub on.

And I didn't disappoint. I grubbed so hard Heckle and Jeckle turned off the TV to watch me eat. They observed me like a science project and called the spectacle an Olympic sport. I took the comment as a compliment and then chugged the entire gallon of pineapple soda for emphasis. And... dismount. Dad beamed with pride. Since I wasn't the athlete son he'd hoped for, me eating like one was his consolation prize. We both took whatever crumbs we could get.

I gathered up the wrappers from my Olympic feast and carried them into the kitchen. When I turned around from the trash can, Dad was standing in the doorway holding a jewelry box. He told me he loved me more than any possession in the world. He told me he was proud of me. Then he reminded me again that he loved me. Dad's words were tinged with sincerity and guilt. I responded with indifference. It was our normal communication. The jewelry box contained a vintage signet ring. My Dad explained that religious leaders used the ring back in the day to confirm important events and that it was a family heirloom. He wanted me to have it to mark my rite of passage. I hugged his neck and thanked him.

Just as I was about to leave, a young woman showed up wearing an outfit that left little—if anything—to the imagination. Seeing her made me salivate more than the food I'd just devoured. Dad quickly intervened and let me know the afternoon delight wasn't meant for me. Then he ushered Miss Hot Pants through the living room and told me I could see myself out. I left the ring box on the TV tray and drove my horny ass home.

I arrived home from Dad's, still horny, pissed and alone. April and I were currently in off mode, but I called her anyway to see if she was down for some birthday sex. I'd left several messages for her earlier in the week but got radio silence, which was odd because she responded to my calls even when we were on the outs. I hung up the phone when I heard April's answering machine come on.

Then, without thinking, I dialed Peaches' number. She answered on the second ring and sang Happy Birthday after hearing my voice. She told me not to move because she was bringing me my gift and then hung up. I stroked myself and smiled.

Peaches pulled into the driveway 40 minutes later. She exited the car wearing a long, black winter coat tied at the waist. It was September and 78 degrees outside. I stroked myself again. Peaches stepped past the threshold and closed the door behind her.

She opened the coat to reveal her birthday suit with two red bows taped to her nipples. We fucked right there in the entryway. It felt like Halloween and the Fourth of July. A sugar rush with fireworks.

After the festivities, I pulled on my shorts while Peaches shimmied into her coat. We hadn't spoken yet. I stood in the entryway as Peaches walked towards the door.

"You're not going to show me out?" she asked.

"You're not a guest," I responded.

Peaches fiddled with her belt and sighed, "Mylo, I still love you."

I walked over to the door and opened it for her to exit. When she turned around, I said, "Well, that's a damn shame" and slammed the door. The sound was orgasmic.

The day's events weren't exactly the Hallmark card I hoped for, but the phone call I received next beckoned to keep hope alive.

"Happy Birthday Big Pimping! Word on the street is your balls dropped today. Welcome to the big league!" It was my gremlin, Calvin.

"Thanks, man. Feels good to finally be legal to do everything I've been doing since I was 13." I joked.

"So, what's the plan? Who or what you planning to get into for your big day?" Calvin asked.

I laughed into the receiver. "I was hoping you'd tell me. Aren't you supposed to be my fairy godfather or something?"

"Shit, I'm not into fairy dust, but I'm definitely getting you fucked up tonight. You smoke weed?" Calvin questioned.

"Nah, man. I don't get down like that." I answered.

"Whatever, choir boy. You gon' learn tonight. Put your Mickey Mouse ears on and pick me up at my crib at eight. I'm taking you to Disneyland." Calvin hung up before I could respond. I just shook my head. Typical Calvin.

Calvin was a loose cannon and the perfect guy to hang with during my existential birthday crisis. He was three years my senior, had no regard for rules, and a mind that wandered frequently without supervision. Both of our fathers were preachers, so like everything else in the church, we were guilted into association as kids. The real bond of our friendship was that we were both loners who resented our dads. Kindred spirits, so to speak. Calvin worked as a hospital orderly and was married in a shotgun wedding the previous year. I'd played for the wedding and hadn't heard much from him since then. Calvin was one of those people who mysteriously appeared when something heavy was happening. And it was usually a sign some serious shit was about to go down. Like I said, he's my gremlin.

I pulled up to Calvin's apartment at eight sharp. He was outside waiting for me, pacing and talking to himself. He hopped into the passenger seat before I came to a complete stop.

"Man, you looked like you were dressed by elves. You plan on taking a sleigh to Whoville tonight?" Calvin snapped.

"See, I wasn't gone say anything about that PTA starter kit outfit you're rocking." I countered. Calvin laughed and gave me a dap.

"How's wifey doing? Am I a play uncle yet?" I asked.

"Man, Linda's about to pop any day now." Calvin stared out the passenger window. His knee was bouncing a thousand miles a minute.

"What's bothering you, Calvin?" I asked.

"Nouns," Calvin mumbled.

My whole face bunched. "Huh?"

"I said, NOUNS. People, places, things. Shit, didn't you just graduate high school?" Calvin snapped. He was still staring out the passenger window.

"So, everything's bothering you. I get it. Wanna talk about it?

"Nope." His tone was edgy.

"Okay then... Where we heading to, Daddy Daycare?"

"Weed Patch on Jefferson," Calvin responded. His knee stopped bouncing.

"Jefferson? Aww, hell nah! Disneyland, my ass! You must not want me to see the day after 18. What in the holy hell you got going on over there?" I yelled.

"Calm the fuck down, lightweight. I'm just going to pick up some contraband for our festivities. You don't have to get out the car. Just drop me off at the corner, drive around the block, and meet me back there so we can roll. You cool?" Calvin asked. The look he gave me was a dare.

I put the car in drive and pulled away from the curb.

My hands shook the whole ride down Jefferson. This car ride was becoming a prayer meeting. I let Calvin off a block from the Weed Patch as planned. A small crowd was congregating outside doing what hood folk do. I was driving like Mr. Magoo, trying not to draw attention to myself. But all eyes were on me like I didn't belong.

Then a scary-looking dude wearing a wife beater and a diamond cross chain started boring a hole through me. He was reaching for his gun. All of a sudden, I heard a pound on the car. It was Calvin. He opened the car door and screamed, "DRIVE!!!!!!!" I laid on the gas with Calvin still clutching the door handle. He managed to maneuver into the passenger seat, but his shirt was collateral damage.

"I knew I shouldn't have brought your squeaky ass over here! You almost got us shot!" Calvin shrieked.

I was too scared to form a complete sentence. I just kept driving.

We were headed towards downtown a few minutes later when Calvin's beeper went off. It was the hospital. They needed him there ASAP. Linda was in labor.

I made a beeline for the hospital. Calvin was rubbing his head and mouthing to himself in silence. His beeper kept going off.

"Man, aren't you going to check your beeper? Something could be wrong with Linda and the baby."

"It's not Linda. Just get me to the hospital. I want you to come in with me."

I nodded and drove. We made our way to the maternity ward 10 minutes later. Calvin checked in at the nurse's station. But instead of seeing Linda, Calvin went to a pay phone and told me to hang out in the waiting room.

Calvin joined me 30 minutes later looking like a kid whose bike just got stolen. He sat down across from me without making eye contact. His knee was bouncing again, double time. He got up almost as soon as he sat down and started pacing the room. He was having a conversation with himself, and hand gestures flew everywhere. I didn't know whether to interrupt him or watch what happened next. I chose the latter.

After a minute or two, Calvin sat back down next to me. The sigh he let out was unsettling."I need a favor, Mylo. And I don't want you to judge me." he pleaded.

"Is Linda okay? Everything all right with the baby?"

"Yeah, Linda's fine. She's still in labor. It's gonna be a while." Calvin put his head in his hand. I could see his chest heaving. "Listen, man. I need to borrow your car. Like right now." Calvin sounded desperate.

"Sure. You need me to get something for you? Because I'm happy to—"

Calvin interrupted me before I could finish the thought."NO! I don't need you to get anything!" Calvin jumped up and started pacing again. He walked to the other side of the waiting area and kicked one of the chairs.

I darted over and grabbed Calvin's arm. "Let's go outside for a minute. You look like you need some air."

I stepped in front of Calvin to establish eye contact and then led him towards the door. I didn't let go of his arm until we reached the sidewalk outside. "Okay, talk! What's going on that you don't need me to judge? And don't bullshit me, Calvin, I mean it!"

Calvin backed up against the wall and slid to sit down. His head was between his hands.

"I fucked up, man. I mean, *REALLY* fucked up. For real this time." He let out another unsettling sigh. "Bro, you remember Tina? Well, I never quit her when I married Linda, and she's pregnant, too. That's why I need your car. She just gave birth over at Mercy. A boy." Calvin heaved.

"Shit!" I cried. "Is the baby yours?"

"Motherfucker, you been gargling bong water? Yes, the baby's mine. I'm not going over there to play Double Dutch!" Calvin shouted.

"Man, how'd you go from planning one birthday to three?" I broke out laughing. Calvin gave me half a peace sign with both hands.

We sat in silence, trying to digest the situation. After a few minutes, I gave Calvin my car keys and said I'd page him if there were any updates with Linda. Calvin hugged me and headed towards the parking garage. I shook my head and walked back into the hospital. Typical Calvin.

Calvin's wife gave birth 90 minutes later to an eight-pound baby boy. Calvin missed the birth and the ridiculous lie I'd told Linda about him leaving to find a car seat. I didn't know they'd been gifted three.

I took that faux pas as my queue to get out of dodge. I was gonna need rehab and a neck brace if I attempted any more lies with Linda. So, I sent Calvin another 911 page and ordered a pizza delivery. I needed a double pepperoni fix, stat. The circus of today's events had put a Ringling Bros level of stank on my birthday festivities, and my appetite was in overdrive.

I was headed to meet the pizza delivery guy when I saw April's mom standing in front of the elevator doors. "Fuck! Now what?" I whispered to myself. I guess my birthday stank hadn't reached the heavens after all.

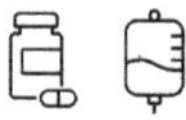

April was in the hospital. She needed a blood transfusion to treat her sickle cell disease and was in a great deal of pain. I listened to April's mom tell me this in total disbelief. How had I not known April was sick? Was I that shitty a boyfriend? Was that why April kept fishing for other guys? And why hadn't April told me? Once again, April's thickening plot had me dazed and confused.

My growling stomach snapped me out of the thought trance. Mrs. Barnes had stopped talking and was looking at me like I was a hospital patient. Then it dawned on me: she had no idea why I was at the hospital. I quickly explained I was there with a friend whose wife just had a baby. Then I asked her to wait while I got my pizza.

When I returned, I offered Mrs. Barnes a slice and asked for April's room number. Visiting hours were over, but I said I'd come back the next day to see April. Mrs. Barnes rattled off the room number, patted my shoulder, and told me to enjoy my pizza. She walked away like the weight of the world was balancing on her shoulders. A Filet-O-Fish wasn't going to fix this situation.

I wasn't prepared for what I saw when I visited April the next day. My Rolls Royce looked like a hoopty. April's face was swollen and unrecognizable. Her stomach was distended like she was six months pregnant. But the worst sight was the light missing in her eyes. April looked like a shell full of misery. I was terrified but forced myself not to show it. I wanted April to see I was a strong man.

Mrs. Barnes was there when I arrived and seemed really impressed with my composure. To keep up the charade, I'd falsely confessed to April's mom I was accustomed to hospitals. I waxed poetic about my Mom's battle with illnesses and how I'd helped take care of her growing up. It wasn't a total lie, at least not the taking care of my mom part. Truthfully, until the night before, I'd never set foot in a hospital.

It must have been a convincing lie, though because Mrs. Barnes' shoulders relaxed, and she gave me her signature smile frown of approval. She told me she always knew I was an admirable young man, then excused herself so April and I could be alone. Mrs. Barnes' words were exactly the balm my flimsy sense of maturity needed.

I sat and watched April sleep for a bit. It was odd hearing her moan from pain instead of pleasure. April's bed at home was a playground. But I'd quickly learn that hospital beds were her truth serum.

"Hey, you. How'd you find out I was here?" April finally noticed I was in the room. Her voice sounded like it needed an oil change.

"Hi! Umm, I was hanging out with my friend Calvin for my birthday last night when his wife went into labor. I stayed until she had the baby and saw your mom as I was leaving. She told me you were here."

"What did they have? A boy or girl?"

"A boy. Over eight pounds. They're both gonna need extra jobs to feed him. Either that, or he'll be the youngest kid ever with a paper route." I joked.

April gave me a weak grin."Tell them I said congratulations. And happy birthday. Sorry, I don't have a gift for you." her face sunk.

"Hey, you getting better is the best present you can give me," I replied.

"About that, Mylo. I don't know how much my mom told you." April sighed and looked at the door.

"Have you ever heard of sickle cell disease?" April asked.

I nodded yes.

"Do you know much about it or anyone who has it?" she continued.

I shook my head "no" to both.

"Well, now you do. This..." April scanned her hand over her body.

"This has been happening to me since I was a little girl, and there's no cure. Sickle cell is a genetic blood disease that affects mainly Black and Brown folks and isn't well understood by a lot of people. Especially people in the medical field. They don't take Black pain seriously, Mylo.

But that's a tale for another day. Let me try and explain what happens." April shifted her weight in the bed and exhaled heavily from the effort.

"So, the red blood cells don't move properly through my body because they have a funny shape." April continued. "You see, normal red blood cells are disc-shaped, but mine are shaped like a C or sickle-shaped. Like the name of the disease." April coughed and shifted a few more times. You could see the discomfort on her face.

"Sorry about that. I just needed a moment. So, where did I leave off? Oh yeah, the cells' weird shape causes buildup and keeps oxygen from traveling through my body. When this happens, I go into crisis." April saw my eyes widen like saucers, and she patted my arm.

"I know. It sounds horrible, and trust me, it is. When I'm in crisis, it feels like my body's on fire, and tiny razor blades are flowing through my veins. I'm okay most of the time, but I have to take extremely strong drugs every day to stabilize the pain. But when I have really bad crisis episodes, like now, I have to be hospitalized for weeks sometimes. The doctors have to give me stronger drugs or a blood transfusion to make me better. I'm waiting to have a transfusion now." April stopped a moment. Her breathing was labored from all the talking.

"Mylo, you also need to know the disease doesn't just affect me physically. It's lonely being sick your whole life." April sighed and stared at the flowers on the window ledge. "Since I was little, I've had issues keeping friends and relationships. The long, unexplained hospital stays make people think I'm a flake. So, they just write me off. But I've never wanted sickle cell to define me, so I don't tell people I have it." April shrugged her shoulders and started picking at a thread in her blanket.

"And when guys I like see how serious the disease is, they jet like Carl Lewis. Especially when they learn I probably won't live to see 50. Nobody wants a girl with a use-by date." April shifted again and winced from the pain.

"So now you know the truth, Mylo. That's my so-called life. And I completely understand if you don't want any part of it. This sickness is

A LOT. But it's my normal, and I'm used to it." April looked directly into my eyes to solidify her point.

I looked back emotionlessly to make mine. "So, your blood's raggedy, and I don't have any sense. We should take a trip to Oz," I teased. I didn't want April to see my pity towards her.

"But seriously, thank you for telling me all that. I know it was hard." I walked over to April and took her hand. "I'm not going anywhere. I believe I'm in love with you, and your illness won't change that."

April smiled and squeezed my hand. At that moment, I realized I wasn't the only one going through growing pains. April was having a growth spurt of her own. She was finally in a relationship with someone who didn't own a pair of track shoes.

Once April got the transfusion, it was night and day. All the swelling disappeared, and she looked like herself again. It was amazing to see how she bounced back after a near-death experience.

April would have numerous more hospital visits like this throughout our relationship together. Each time, she got weaker and weaker, not bouncing back as quickly. As time progressed, I noticed April's family leaned on me more and more to ease the stress of her hospital stays on them. April had finally caught her whale.

## Culture Shock

Cultural conditioning. Besides money, it's the root of all evil. It taints our perceptions of people, places, events... and worst of all—love. If you think about it, cultural norms are nothing more than sanctioned bad advice that keeps us looking for love in all the wrong places. Especially if you're a guy.

Society has men believing that whole alpha male, caretaker-of-the-weaker sex bullshit. Men hunt and gather attention, sex, and pity and confuse it for a standardized notion of love. The aftermath is generations of clueless guys (with Captain Save-a-Hoe mentalities) lost on having their egos stroked rather than what makes their hearts smile. It's what happens when a dog chases its tail and finally catches it.

I'd been chasing my tail with April for over a year. It was an unrequited love affair that had me so emotionally constipated I hadn't given a shit about myself in months. I'd bounced from boyhood to manhood, Peaches to April, self-doubt to self-blame, and been charmed and dick stroked into becoming a rescuer for everyone except my damn self. Yet, I was too whipped to realize the view's better when you pull your head out of your ass. All that tail chasing had spun my life into a heaping pile of dog shit.

I still had my organist job at the church and even enrolled (then dropped out of) junior college. School just wasn't for me. I didn't have the attention span for intellectualism, so catering to April became my full-time job. And trust me, being in love with April Barnes was an exhausting j-o-b.

Although I'd turned a blind eye to April's illness and gave her my heart on a platter, it hadn't changed a damn thing. April's fishing for male attention became her game of choice. She'd toss me out for a new catch, then bait me back in whenever the spirit led her.

Her latest catch of the day was Craig Lumbar. Craig was a local news reporter with a face for radio. I'm pretty sure Chess King sponsored his news copy because he wore every outfit featured in their display windows. April loved it. April loved anything shiny and new.

Anyway, the Craig and April train crashed and burned three months into the relationship. April had one of her hospital stints, and Newsboy couldn't take the heat. I was beyond excited when April asked to see me once the ashes cooled. When I got to her apartment, it was like the first time we met. No words, just lots of body language and heavy breathing. I pledged allegiance to her freak flag (once again), and we ended up back together. In hindsight, I know this was a HUGE mistake. But at the time, I was smelling myself and didn't fully understand self-worth. I only knew how to take the blame for other people's behavior.

April's demeanor towards me did a complete 180 once we reconciled. It's like my unconditional love triggered her into bitch mode. Nothing I did or said mattered or pleased her. She was demanding, impatient, and belittling, and my presence around her felt like a giant chastisement. April finally told me I wasn't being responsible and needed to figure out what I wanted to do in life so we could live better. She wasn't wrong. My identity had been wrapped up in being mature for my age. But here I was with no purpose and my shame becoming a burden. I was at a crossroads and needed to talk to someone. But I'd ignored everyone's warnings about my involvement with April, so I was alone in the hole I'd dug. Shit, I couldn't even talk to the person I'd dug the hole for! I felt fucked in the worst possible way.

Most people in my situation get discouraged from believing they've exhausted all their options. My problem was I didn't know what my options were. And in my opinion, that's far more debilitating. I needed a new response to my analysis paralysis. That response turned out to be April's Dad.

Todd Barnes was a man's man. He got along with everyone from the gutter to the board room and doled out great advice like Cracker Jack prizes. He owned a nightclub, ran a sports center, and NEVER lost his cool. Living in a house full of daughters and dealing with knuckleheaded athletes daily kept him grounded. I admired how upstanding he was. So, of course, he was the natural choice to help me make sense of my life.

I popped in on Mr. Barnes early one Saturday morning. I knew he'd be out tending to the grass, and we'd have time to ourselves. He smiled when I arrived and handed me a rake. He believed in staying busy and was meticulous with his lawn. We worked in silence for a good five minutes before either of us spoke.

"You know, Mylo, life's as random as it is deliberate. Which side of life does this visit reside on?" Mr. Barnes probed.

"Ahh, I see Yoda got an early start on his caffeine fix today," I teased. "But sir, I'm afraid I'm such a disaster the Red Cross wouldn't offer me any coffee," I replied.

"Aww, so the answer is C. Existential." Mr. Barnes took the rake from my hand and motioned for me to sit down.

"You might say that, sir," I told Mr. Barnes how frustrated I was with life. I described how it felt like I needed to be doing something but didn't know what. I'd just dropped out of a police academy program and contemplated becoming a fireman. I was scheduled to take the written exam and wasn't even sure about that. I was a question mark looking for answers.

Mr. Barnes listened to me with his eyes closed. "Well, Mylo, it sounds like you made the right decision regarding not becoming a police officer. And I think you also need to give this dream of becoming a fireman a good thought. You mean to tell me you want to run into a burning building that people are running out of to put out a fire? Think about that." Mr. Barnes put his elbows on the armrests and leaned forward to look me in the eyes.

"Mylo, I promise that you'll figure this out one way or another. I was once in your shoes, and I figured it out. And I have faith that you will as well. Don't worry about school. Pshaw! School isn't for everyone, you know. Some people love to learn but hate to be taught. Look, you're very talented and an extremely hard worker. Your success doesn't need to come from books. When I was your age, I joined the Air Force. It was the best time of my life! Picture it, Okinawa, 1963..." Mr. Barnes went full Sophia from *Golden Girls* on me for the next two and a half hours. He told me story after story about all the places and adventures he'd been on around the world. I ate it up like Charlie at the chocolate factory, chilling with the Oompa Loompas. His words were my golden ticket, and I was completely spellbound.

So much so that I signed up to join the Air Force.

I contemplated for a month whether or not I wanted to go through with my decision to join the Air Force. I'd officially moved in with April, and the relationship had turned serious. *Too* serious.

April was asking questions about whether or not I was going to marry her. She still hadn't said she loved me. The stress of all the potential life changes at once was more than my 19-year-old brain could handle. I still didn't know what I wanted to do in life, and I didn't want to lose April. My crossroad had six lanes of traffic.

April Barnes was a complicated being. A mixture of cupcakes and rainbows, mischief, and SpaghettiOs. Although she was eight years my senior, she had the temperament and attention span of a spoiled rotten three-year-old. When April didn't get her way or felt backed into a corner, she went into these dramatic, fake crying fits to defeat the situation. Her sister Brenda told me once that April had been using the fake tears since she was a kid and never grew out of it. Along with her illness, it was the emotional blackmail April leveraged as her superpower. Unfortunately for me, tears were my kryptonite.

After some time, there was a change of guard in our relationship, and I was no longer royalty. April was calling the shots, and I was being relegated to servitude. The change was subtle and then abrupt. Like looking both ways to cross the street, then getting hit by a plane. In my defense, I was young and focused on appearances. Transfixed on wanting to be in a relationship and April saying and doing all the right things. I was only considering the short-term outcomes, not the intentions. I didn't even realize I'd been isolated and trapped.

I was sitting on the couch with April one Sunday after church, and the marriage question came up again. April announced if we were going to get married, I needed to ask her father for her hand. In a nutshell, April had decided we were getting married for both of us. It was her usual modus operandi. My confusion, reluctance, and fear of losing her if I differed made my timid ass say okay.

Before my butt cheeks could leave an indent on the couch cushion, April got me up and dragged me to her parents' house. When we got there, her entire family was waiting for us in the dining room. April's sister, Danielle, had flown in from North Carolina, and everyone was grinning like kids gawking in a toy store window.

April sat me across from Mr. Barnes at the dining room table while the rest of the family mysteriously disappeared. I was nervous, but Mr. Barnes was very considerate and patiently listened as I squeaked my request for April's hand in marriage. He looked at me and asked if I was sure this was what I wanted to do. I stared back like a deer in headlights and mumbled a weak yes. I exhaled, thinking I was off the hook. I went to put my hand on the table to stand up when Mr. Barnes asked me what my plan was. I folded my hands, straightened my back, and told him I was joining the Air Force. He smiled so hard I thought his face would crack. At least I'd done something right. Mr. Barnes took a moment to compose himself, then told me he doesn't get involved in his children's business when it comes to their relationships. His girls were all grown and had to sleep with their spouses, not him.

After a pause, Mr. Barnes sighed and asked me to treat April with love and respect. I agreed and officially got his blessing.

The whole family instantly reappeared after Mr. Barnes and I hugged it out. Then, from out of nowhere, April showed me her grandmother's ring and said that we would take it to the mall to trade it in for a ring for her. Before I could blink, I was whisked off to a jewelry store where April had the ring she wanted, waiting for her to try it on.

I headed back to the jeweler a week later and got the ring. Afterward, I went straight to April's apartment, where she was waiting for me. I pulled out the ring and said, "Will," she screamed "YES!!!!"

at the top of her lungs, then went into a fake crying episode. I was in a daze as she called what seemed like a hundred people to tell them she was engaged. Afterward, we went to her parents' house, where a party was already in motion to celebrate our engagement. The trap was now a barricade.

They say most leaps of faith are preceded by a shove. I was parked in front of the Air Force recruiter's office at 7 am the next morning. I'd been dropped-kicked into putting on my big boy pants and couldn't hold off on my decision any longer.

The recruiter saw me in my car, came outside, and waved me in. I walked over to his desk and sat down. Sergeant Ruth sat on the corner of his desk and looked at me like a wayward child.

"Son, tell me. What do you want to do?" Sergeant Ruth asked.

"I honestly don't know." I was having a staring contest with the floor.

"Well, it's been a month, Mylo. But the decision is yours. Can I give you a piece of advice?"

I nodded, still staring at the carpet.

"Don't be someone who regrets a chance you didn't take. You're not doing anything and don't want to go to college. You're 19, right?"

I nodded again.

"Okay, so you're young and have a blank slate ahead. Look, we have this new bid where you serve three years of active duty and seven years non-active. That means the Air Force could call you back into active duty for up to seven years if needed. It's a good option for someone like you to get a taste of the world. Again, the choice is yours." Sergeant Ruth walked around to his chair and sat down.

I got up and paced around the office. I'd just agreed to be someone's husband but hadn't lived. This could be my only chance to find myself.

I turned around and faced Sergeant Ruth. "Fuck it! Sign me up!" I finally decided to take ownership of my life. I was finally going to be a MAN.

## Booty Call

I was scheduled to leave for boot camp in two weeks. I told April I wasn't telling anyone I was leaving. Not even my Mom. I just wanted to up and go, then surprise everyone when I came home a REAL man.

The night before I left for boot camp, I was in the bedroom, taking a nap. Suddenly, the lights came on, and my Mom was nudging me awake. April had called her over. Mom hugged and rocked me for what felt like an eternity. The last time she'd hugged me like that was when she and my Dad split. I just hoped I wouldn't be entering combat before I reached boot camp.

"Air Force, huh? Do you know where you'll be stationed?" Mom was ready to talk.

"No, not yet. I'll be in San Antonio, Texas, for boot camp and get my orders afterward. Mom, are you mad at me for not telling you?" I felt like I was five all over again.

"Oh, Mylo. Do you know how hard it is to see a burning building and not yell fire?" she sighed heavily and patted my cheek.

"No, I'm not mad, Mylo. You're an adult, and I respect your decisions always. You're responsible for your happiness, not me. Are you happy, Mylo?" I could see tears forming in Mom's eyes.

"I think I am, Mom. This feels like my only opportunity to take charge of my life. You know, get some structure." I paused and climbed out of bed.

"Did April tell you our other news?" I was facing the wall. I couldn't look Mom in the eye.

"No, she just told me you were leaving for boot camp tomorrow and thought I should see you before you left. There's more?" she asked.

"April and I are engaged. It happened a few weeks ago. April really wants us to get married." I was still looking at the wall.

"I see. Well, congratulations, son." Mom walked over and put her hand on my shoulder. "You said April wants the two of you to get married. Do you want that, too?" Mom's voice was calm and sincere.

All I could do was shrug. Mom didn't push for more. She told me she loved me, and I began to melt. We hugged, and I was off to boot camp the next morning.

Boot camp was the best, worst thing I've ever done. Like going in raw and coming out with a condom. Until this point, I thought shame, resistance, and resentment were my rock bottom. Then, I encountered basic training and the process of breaking a guy down to build him back up. The basics were physical, mental, and emotional. The training got those houses in order to develop someone so big and bad that people (and all their weapons of malintent) couldn't touch you. As fucked up as it may sound, the Air Force was the communal father-son relationship I needed to grow up. I was finally independent, away from selfish women and my own isolation. It equipped me to battle life as a fully realized man.

When the bus dropped us off at boot camp, I tried to turn around and get back on it. But the bus driver shut the door in my face and shouted, "Suck it the fuck up!" before driving off. I felt like a cat on a screen door.

My company commander, Chief Huxley, was a 5'4" bag of insults who road my ass like Seabiscuit. And I'd given him full permission to saddle up.

Chief Huxley took one look at me and yelled, "Gunn, I'm gonna get all of that jelly belly off your fat ass! You're gonna run until those hotdogs on the back of your neck fall off! And if I tell you to eat a bushel of fruit, you better shit me out a fruit salad!"

Chief Huxley's jabs should have made me madder than a toothless vampire. But instead, they quietly made me smile. I was thrilled to finally be in a controlled program to lose weight. Not just when my self-esteem was low. My transformation from buffet to Happy Meal was shocking. I went in weighing 225 pounds. and left six weeks later weighing 149 pounds. My own mother didn't recognize me when she came to my graduation. This grooming felt respectable and empowering.

My squadron nicknamed me Baby Grand. And not just because I played the piano. They envied my ability to favorably manipulate situations like those 88 keys. Like convincing the Air Force personnel that I could perform training with my civilian glasses instead of the birth control glasses the military issued. I don't know exactly what I said or did to weasel my way out of it, but it worked... temporarily.

I cracked my civilian glasses two weeks into basic training and was running around blind as a bat. Every night, I prayed to Jesus, Muhammad, Buddha, and Vishnu to heal my vision and avoid the inevitable.

But Chief Huxley saw me faking the funk and made plans to check my ass. He ordered me to his office one afternoon after drills. I stood at attention in front of his desk, sweating like a fat hooker in church.

"Gunn, I've been having so much fun turning your ass into a Happy Meal that I want to give you a gift of appreciation." Chief Huxley gave me a sideways smirk. I felt my butt cheeks clench from the fuckery about to go down.

"Gunn, let me see those Guess designer baby maker spectacles you're wearing." Chief was grinning like a Cheshire cat now.

I removed my glasses and placed them on the edge of his desk.

Chief picked up the glasses and twirled them in between his fingers. I tried not to gulp.

"Yes, these are mighty fine, indeed," the twirling continued. "But I've got something I think you'll like even better." Chief sat my glasses in the middle of his desk, reached behind him, then put his hands behind his back.

"From now on, you're going to wear these!" Chief positioned his hands in front of him, holding the biggest, ugliest pair of space modulator eyeglasses you've ever cringed at. "Now you'll be able to see *ALL* the women unwilling to fuck your fat ass."

The other cadets roasted me like a marshmallow for the next three days. They even taped a carwash ticket to my locker to get my glasses cleaned. I don't know what was more challenging to survive—boot camp or losing my vanity to those hideous windshields I was forced to wear.

Boot camp was as confusing as it was gratifying. Gratifying in the sense that I'd physically and emotionally transformed into a more fit and confident version of myself. Confusing because despite distance and time, the accomplishment was still being micromanaged by April's involvement.

I was extremely excited about starting a new life in a different part of the world. But that opportunity got kicked to the curb because of April's illness and our impending marriage. Instead of my original orders in Guam, the Air Force stationed me in the States. The expression ball and chain had never felt more real.

April was thrilled I'd joined the Air Force. I was young, fit, employed, and poised to protect and serve. It was the perfect spit polish finish to her grooming regimen. She and my Mom attended my basic training graduation, and I was excited to see their familiar faces. After the ceremony, I immediately spotted Mom and held back the urge to run to her like an anxious kid. April gave me a jealous, stank eye for hugging Mom first. I knew I'd pay for the impulse later.

At the hotel, April prattled on about the wedding. She'd already planned every detail. I just needed to choose the best man and show up in my military uniform. I smiled, nodded, and listened for my name. I'd contributed too much psychological debt to care about wedding plans. April eventually paused and asked if I was having cold feet. She changed the subject before I could answer.

I thought about calling off the wedding more than a few times. Hell, a part of me thinks it's what got me through boot camp: the opportunity to be free-range while serving my country was well within my grasp. I'll admit the notion excited and terrified me. But so did marrying April. April deserved to be loved. And apparently, I was the only person willing to give her that unconditionally. What can I say? Codependency is a hell of a drug.

The wedding happened two days after I returned home from ops training. The whole thing was a complete blur, and I honestly don't remember that much. At least 350 people attended the ceremony. I brought a guy from my squadron to be my best man (I forget his name). Cedric coordinated the music, cake was eaten, and everyone played their respective roles.

My only vivid memory from the day was a note April taped to the garment bag holding my military dress uniform before the ceremony. I remember removing the tape and silently hoping that April had written me a mushy love note.

To my disappointment, it was a scrap piece of paper instructing me to rub Vaseline on my teeth to make it easier to smile throughout the ceremony. The word "love" didn't appear anywhere in the note.

I don't recall what April looked like walking down the aisle. Nor do I recollect having any groom-like emotions, like anticipation or excitement. I just remember the taste of Vaseline and that damn note reminding me that our wedding day, like everything else in our relationship, had absolutely nothing to do with me.

Two weeks after the wedding, I reported to my duty station in Santa Barbara, California, and the wedding bells suddenly became warning bells.

## People Need People

Connections are a strange paradigm. They provide a sense of purpose, belonging, fulfillment, and quality of life. The connective tissue from knee bone to hip bone, feeling to thought, and action to interaction is essential for the survival of the fittest. Its comfort serves as both a blessing and a curse. It provides a floor but also a ceiling. While love has no boundaries, connections are transactional acts that tie and bind but also break. That's why love connections are such horrible hazards.

Military life in Santa Barbara was good for me. The beach, ambiguity, and military assignments in any given country were the exploratory learning I needed. And my journey towards alpha male-dom had taught me a LOT.

For starters, I learned the military's a fucked-up brotherhood. One where everybody's an asshole and full of shit by default. There's an expectation of tripping over tradition to avoid thinking for yourself, and being dysfunctional is damn near a requirement. It's a circle of life where confidence is born, relationships die, and the other shoe always drops. And in Santa Barbara, it rained shoes like a motherfucker.

I felt the first shoe drop in my station orientation. I must have done something horrible in my previous life because I reported to Chief Huxley—yet again. Yes, that glasses-stealing Freddie Kruger with a Napolean complex was back to make Friday the 13th an everyday occurrence. My birth control glasses fogged up every time Chief entered the room.

Chief Huxley was a bit of an anomaly. A Filipino man with a Southern accent, a face like Cheech Marin, and Mr. Miyagi sensibilities. He made for a hard read at any given moment, and this particular moment was no exception. Chief waxed on and off about duties and expectations when things got interesting.

"How many of you asshats are married?" Chief Huxley paced the length of the office looking for blood pressures to raise. I sheepishly held up my hand. High blood pressure already ran in my family. "So, almost half of you are institutionalized, I see. Well, let me peep you to a little something. That wedding ring you got on is no kryptonite against all the pussy about to be thrown at you working for Uncle Sam."

I saw eyes widening like saucers all around me.

"You think these little single punks are gonna get all the ass while you're in here? Think again, my bitch ass betrothed. These women want Sergeant Lonely Heart and his wedding band. They're coming for YOU!" Chief pointed at the Airman sitting beside me, twisting his wedding ring.

"You're the forbidden fruit these women wanna fuck and suck. So get ready to swing, batter, batter, swing. Because a big part of your assignment around here will be beating off pussy with a bat." We all looked around at each other, uncertain how (or whether) to react.

"Especially you, Happy Meal." Chief stopped in front of me with one eyebrow raised. "Someone big and Black like you, Gunn, is gonna attract more pussy than all of us combined." Chief bent down and met me eyeball to eyeball. "So choke up on your swing and break in your catcher's mitt, Jackie Robinson. It's about to be the world series up in here." Chief straightened up, tipped his hat, and paced in the opposite direction.

I didn't know if I wanted to salute or scratch my head. My commanding Chief had just issued me a hall pass.

I was slowly settling into my new life in Santa Barbara. I found an apartment, was playing the organ for a local church, and the guys in my unit were the Marco to my Polo for everything in between. My new little community was shaping up nicely. All that was missing was my new wife. Cue: shoe drop #2...

When someone says, "You've changed," it really means you've stopped conducting life *their* way. April had mixed feelings about moving to Santa Barbara. She'd never lived outside a two-mile radius of her parents' reach or a doctor's orders and made both points abundantly clear.

She argued daily that life alone with me would leave her gasping for air. I should have taken her dramatic response as a warning. But relationships for me had always been a love pat followed by a sucker punch, so I didn't let April's ambivalence get to me.

But when she called me the day before her move to Santa Barbara to say she wouldn't be coming to live there —EVER—I was wrecked.

Despite appearances, family and health weren't April's issues. It was money. More specifically, how little she felt I was making. Understand, April was a pampered princess whose family had given her *Officer and a Gentleman* expectations. So when she realized she'd married Gilligan instead of Richard Gere's movie character, shit hit the fan—HARD.

April couldn't... no, *wouldn't* understand that I was young, had barely graduated high school, and was considered a peon in the military. You see, logic didn't exist with April. She only understood what she wanted. nothing. else. mattered. I was simply around to protect and serve the means to her end. And the fact that I deposited almost my entire check into April's account every month (I kept only $100 for myself) didn't win me any brownie points. I was the poster child for "damned if I do or don't".

I sat and listened to April's beratement through the phone receiver while tears rolled down my cheeks. Her money digs towards me were cutting, cruel, and without apology.

When she finished, I told her I understood and would let the Air Force know I'd be flying solo. I didn't have enough strength or ego to argue.

She offered me a consolation prize of flying to California once a month when I wasn't on assignment.

All I could muster was, "Sure, that would be great," while I wiped my face. Being a military spouse wasn't turning out to be the "Aim High" experience I'd signed up for.

But I'd made my bed. I just wasn't prepared to lay in it alone.

April kept her word and visited me monthly for the next three months. She'd stay four days at a pop, and we made the most of our visits. Of course, there was plenty of action between the sheets. We were fine there. But we also took in the sights. Trips to the zoo, strolls along Stearns Wharf, chasing windmills in Solvang... Our time together was picturesque and petty. Because despite the hugs and kisses, fun and sun, all of our interactions ended up in arguments about money. Endless squabbles about my ineptness to earn enough and April's desire for more of everything. It was the exclamation point on our marriage deal.

Our unit was issued a six-month assignment in Australia, and I was REALLY geeked. Serving and protecting alongside kangaroos and koalas was a rollercoaster and a dream I couldn't wait to experience. We learned we'd spend most of our assignment in Perth and had less than 24 hours before departing. Little did I know this would be the shoe that would break the camel's back.

I called April to tell her about my new assignment after we landed in Australia. This was in 1990, which meant I had to dial an operator using a calling card to get an international connection. Kind of like a collect call from prison. In hindsight, the irony of that makes sense now.

Anyway, it was 4 pm in Perth, meaning it was 3 am in Buffalo. When the operator patched me through, a man answered the phone. I responded with a stream of questions and expletives that made my own ears bleed. The phone operator laughed indiscreetly on the other line. I knew then I was the punchline in the situation.

I was completely mortified and didn't know what to do. I stopped mid-sentence and slammed down the phone. How could April do this?

Fuming, I paced back and forth like a caged animal, then called April's sister, Brenda.

"Mylo, what's wrong?" Brenda croaked into the receiver.

"Brenda, I just called April, and some dude answered the phone! You know what's going on?" I yelled.

There was dead silence on the other end of the line. It felt like a silent kick to my nut sacks.

"I'm sorry, Mylo. I don't know what you want me to say." Brenda let out a labored sigh.

"Heifer, you know? Wooww! Ain't this some shit! So what happened? Huh? Tell me! What the hell's going on?" Saliva was spewing out of my mouth. I could feel my nostrils flare.

"Mylo, I'm sorry. I don't know what else to say. I'm so, so, sorry." Brenda paused for several seconds. "Jesus Christ." she whispered. "Mylo, if you want to know more, call my mom. I'm sorry."

I heard a click, then silence. Brenda hung up. FUCK! If I ever needed speed dial, it was now.

I stared at the receiver, confused and shaking. What was happening?

"These international phone operators gone earn their checks today!" I yelled at the empty room in front of me before picking up the phone again.

Mrs. Barnes didn't sound surprised by my call. I told her the same thing I'd told Brenda.

"Oh dear, I'm sorry. Really, I am. I thought Mimi would be content with you. I honestly did. I didn't know this would happen." Mrs. Barnes sighed. I heard her slippers shuffling across the floor. Then I heard several flicks. She was lighting a cigarette.

"I'm truly sorry, Mylo. But Mimi's being taken care of. That's what matters, right? She's got you taking care of her from there, and Chad's here. *That's* what matters." It sounded like Mrs. Barnes was talking to herself and no one in particular. She did that when she smoked.

All I could think was, dammit, he's got a name.

"Mylo dear, you'll be fine. You'll see. Plenty of people are there with you, so you're good. But Mimi has to be taken care of. Don't you agree?" There was a smile in Mrs. Barnes' voice that made my eye twitch.

I couldn't tell if it was from the nicotine at three in the morning or her mind unhinging. Regardless, it wasn't right. I felt bile building up in my throat.

"So, his name's Chad," I whispered. It was the only thing I could think of saying. Chad. The name was clipped and hard with no feeling in it, probably like his dick.

"Mylo, I'm sorry, honey." Mrs. Barnes continued before her smoker's cough kicked in. The word "honey" registered like a slap. There was nothing sweet about her apology.

"You want me to tell April you called?" Mrs. Barnes asked once her cough subsided.

I was numb. I'd forgotten why I'd called and where I was. I don't even remember responding or hanging up the phone. The world simply went black.

Someone once said "I'm sorry" isn't an apology; it's a habitual way of restoring balance to a conversation. It was true. The responses towards me that afternoon were those of someone who'd been abused: nothing but empty apologies.

April's cheating introduced me to a lot of uncertainties I didn't know on a first-name basis. Like black sheep relatives or people you don't respect but must be polite to for appearances. It was an unthinkable situation that was unsettling and unavoidable. But Chief Huxley constantly reminded our platoon that when the unthinkable happens, you learn about what you can't control and put that knowledge to work. Never would I have imagined that logic would apply to my personal life. But here I was, putting in the work to become a world-class wise ass in my situation with April, and the results weren't pretty.

Psychology suggested my marriage to April was a mama substitute for emotional security. My African peeps believed the younger man-older woman relationships robbed his youth and restored her beauty. A Chinese proverb compared cheating on a good person to throwing away a diamond and picking up a stone. That one gave a whole new twist on the expression "kick rocks." And since I'm a preacher's kid, I sought advice on my marital mishap from our Base Chaplain. But instead of parables and prayers, the Chaplain offered up a recent story about his wife of 20-plus years cheating on him.

She was a kindergarten teacher who'd gotten high using markers in an unventilated room, then turned around and fucked the janitor who rescued her. Talk about teacher's pet. I wound up consoling the Chaplain instead of the reverse. Shit, if a man of God couldn't reconcile his wife's cheating on him, I figured God's grace wouldn't be sufficient enough for me. At this point, I was straddling the fence between choosing the high road and completely disregarding social responsibility. It was a consequential inbetweenness that had me confused as a goat on astroturf. But I figured everything would be copacetic as long as I wore a cup when riding that fence. That was until my friend Goodwin found me having mixed drinks about my feelings and set me straight.

My first encounter with Denny Goodwin felt like fate, cruelty, and catharsis. It was during my first week in Santa Barbara. I'd just wrapped training for the day and was walking towards the elevator when I heard a voice shout, "Hey, Fat Daddy!" I turned around, and Goodwin walked towards me, waving and grinning like a drunk possum.

"Hey, do I know you?" I asked.

"Nope. I just yelled Fat Daddy to see if anyone would turn around. Tag, you're it, Fat Daddy," he responded.

"You motherfucker." I broke out laughing.

"My name's Goodwin. I just got my first orders here in Santa Barbara." Goodwin reached out to shake hands. His palms were the fattest I'd ever seen.

"Got damn, you've got some big hands! You grow up palming watermelons?" I exclaimed.

"You've got a lot to say for someone who answers to Fat Daddy. And I grew up palming ass for your information. These hands were built for asses that look like they've been shoplifting throw pillows." Goodwin's sideways smirk spoke volumes.

"That's a whole lotta information," I chuckled. "You married?" I asked.

"Well, you went from Fat Daddy to Curious George in record time. You should see a shrink about that. Tell you what. Let's find a place that serves milk and cookies and I'll answer anything you want to know. Meet me back here in 20 minutes." Goodwin walked to the elevator and yelled, "Fat Daddy!" as the doors slid closed. All I could do was shake my head.

We were each other's ride-or-die from that point on.

Denny Goodwin was an odd oxymoron: an ex-gang banger from Peoria who, like unbiased opinions and clear misunderstandings, didn't quite make sense. Goodwin was the kind of stereotype that made him both a leader and an outsider. His IQ rivaled his street savvy in this weird mash-up of Rain Man meets Sopranos that came across as more humblebrag than a threat. And the ladies loved him. He claimed to have joined the military to escape being cock-blocked by the streets. According to him, women needed a carrot and a stick and the Air Force uniform gave him just the right dangle.

Goodwin followed me to a local Perth watering hole a few days after my world imploded with April. I was looking for answers at the bottom of a Long Island iced tea when I felt something hit me on the side of the head. I looked up and saw Goodwin standing at the end of the bar, chucking peanuts at me.

"What's good, Fat Daddy? Everything okay? You look like someone shit in your cheerios." Goodwin pulled up a stool while I stabbed at an ice cube in my glass.

"Not now, Goodwin. My mind's wandering." I snapped.

"Well, I can wait until your internal compass kicks in." Goodwin swiveled in his seat. "Hey, can I get a Jack and Ginger?" Goodwin asked the bartender.

I was still playing whack-a-mole with my ice cubes, trying to act like Goodwin wasn't there. He turned towards me and put his knuckles under his chin. His gaze felt like a heat gun on the side of my face.

And since I didn't want to end up in the burn unit, I took a sip of my drink and let the alcohol do the talking. I spilled everything: April, Chad, Brenda, Mrs. Barnes, the money shame, my daddy issues... By the time I shut up, I'd polished off my third Long Island iced tea.

Goodwin leaned back from the bar and looked at me like something stank. "That's some drama and a headache," he huffed.

I pursed my lips in a thin line and turned away. I'd just laid my soul on the bar, and this ass crack was clowning me.

Goodwin placed his hand on my shoulder. I immediately jerked my arm away.

"Damn! It's a joke, not a dick, bro. Don't take it so hard." Goodwin snorted.

I turned around and sighed. I was all out of words.

"Look, Gunn, I'm sorry you've had to go through all of this shit. Whoever said love don't cost a thing can kiss the blackest half of both our asses." He took a long drag from his drink and pushed it aside.

"Love's a fucking loan shark. And it sounds like all the love in your life has given you a shit ton of bad interest. Listen, you ain't obligated to give folks multiple shots at fucking you over. Ya hear me? Your wife's playing chess, not checkers, with your ass. And it's not the fucking game you signed up for." Goodwin spoke the truth with his whole chest.

I nodded and chomped a piece of ice to choke down the reality. "I hear you, Goodwin. But bro, I'm trying to be grown."

I was suddenly out of ice and places to hide. "April's my WIFE, and this shit ain't high school." I stammered. "This right here is my fucked-up life with a security clearance and grown-ass consequences. Hell, I went into this mess trying to be a fucking hero and wound up an anecdote." I paused and let my arms drop. "But dude, I don't want to be petty."

Goodwin shifted his weight towards me and pointed his finger at my chest. "That's the problem with you, Fat Daddy. You're. Too. Nice." His finger jabbed at my chest with each syllable.

"All that lake effect snow has dulled your edge." Goodwin rolled up his sleeve, exposing his Vice Lord tattoo.

"Shit, sometimes being petty is the only way to settle a situation, Gunn. But believe me when I tell you, you're not petty, you're pedagogic."

I couldn't hide my astonishment from the 50-cent word drop.

"Yeah, snow globe, I got a big vocabulary to go with this huge dick-tionary I'm toting." Goodwin pointed at his crotch and flashed his signature half-grin. I could tell the Jack and Ginger was kicking in.

"Listen, Fat Daddy, I've watched you in our unit. You're not a hothead or a fighter; you're a fucking teacher. You analyze. Yeah, then you finesse the shit out of situations like a neutralizer, so you come out on top."

Goodwin stopped and stared at a bottle of Paul Masson before continuing. "You need to checkmate her ass."

♘♖ ♙

I've learned there's a fine line between being petty and pedagogic. Both teach a lesson, but one's stealth and the other has principles. I needed both. A quiet way to settle the score and have some standards without looking like an asshole. Some would call that mean-spirited. But shit, I needed a win. I was nothing more than a squirrel in April's world, and she had me by the nuts. I wanted a release. Something to reset my mind and liberate my ego from the resentment, heartbreak, and blue balls I was dealing with. So I defaulted to my trauma-bonded safe space: Sex.

The hoe phase was Goodwin's idea. He called it personal growth experiential learning. Whatever that means. Said getting over on someone by getting under someone new was a time-tested home remedy. "Like chicken soup for your ego. It's time you answered the military call to booty, Fat Daddy!"

Goodwin argued that since I'd advanced from cradle to honeymoon suite with no in-between, I was entitled to the global fuckfest the military offered. The timing couldn't have been better. We were scheduled to leave for Sydney, Australia, in a few days, and Goodwin offered to be my tour guide to sow some oats. And that he did.

When our aircraft carrier pulled into the pier in Sydney, the women were lined up like they were jockeying for job interviews. All of them beautiful and prime for picking. Australia was the ultimate chessboard of opportunity as the only country in the world covering an entire continent. And I was taking it all in: the beautiful port, all that feminine energy, the unsolicited attention, my nerves... Goodwin saw me sweating like a nomad with a mortgage and pulled me aside. He assured me I'd done my part in being faithful to April. Stressed that since April had taken advantage of my faithfulness, I had the green light to take in everything that came to me. He pointed to the sea of women smiling with their cleavage bouncing in the breeze. I squared my shoulders, took a deep breath, and marched my horny ass toward all those Queens waiting to take my Pawn.

Goodwin and I went out to a club that night. It was the perfect distraction. Vegas on steroids with a five to one woman/man ratio. A place where insecurity is normalized to dysfunctional levels of misery loves company. I dubbed it my new happy place because Disney World had nothing on this.

I danced, drank, and cavorted until I passed out. I was taking my hoe phase seriously and didn't care if that freedom came with a cover charge.

My first checkmate's name was Ivy—as in poison (her words, not mine). She asked if I wanted her to make me itch before we scratched one out in the parking lot. I don't remember Ivy's face, but her hair smelled like bubblegum and lost inhibitions. Being itchy never felt so damn good.

The rest of the evening was a complete blur, though. I do know that I went big, but I didn't go home.

The next morning, I woke up in bed with a stunning Irish girl staring at me. She had dirty blonde hair, periwinkle eyes, and a constellation of freckles across her face. I thought I was dead or dreaming. Either way, life never looked so good.

I wasn't sure of the protocol in this kind of situation, so I nervously extended my hand and said, "Hi, I'm Mylo."

Her giggly response sounded like sunshine and new beginnings. She told me her name was Saoirse, which is Irish for freedom. I saw it as a serendipitous sign for my new hoe phase and thanked the Irish gods for their blessing.

Saoirse told me I'd passed out at the club, and she'd brought me home. She assured me that everything was cool. Goodwin was camped out at her girlfriend's house, and we'd meet up with them later in the day. She sensed my relief and kissed the top of my head.

I noticed her nipple slip out from beneath the bed sheet and immediately looked under the covers: we were both butt-ass naked! Stunned (and seemingly impressed), I asked Saoirse if we'd had sex.

She gave me a sheepish grin and cooed in her breathy Irish accent, "Yes, love. Multiple times, and it was REALLY amazing."

My internal reaction was somewhere between a high five and wanting to shit the bed. I didn't have the heart to tell her I didn't remember any of it. So I kissed her on the forehead and thought of playing connect the dots on her freckles with my tongue.

Then reality jolted me back to my senses. "Hey! Did we use protection?" I asked. She opened her nightstand (three open foil wrappers were lying on top) and showed me a drawer full of condoms. My audible sigh of relief made her giggle again. The memory of the moment still makes me hard.

We made good use of the condom drawer again, then sat in bed and talked for a while before Saoirse got up to make breakfast. It gave me a sense of déjà vu that triggered me a bit. Flashbacks of my first rendezvous with April danced with pitchforks in my head. The recall was painful—like hemorrhoids. I got up and looked for the bathroom. I needed to piss away the past.

Saoirse's place was lovely. Warm and homey, with lots of windows and natural elements. The unfamiliar felt good. I found my way back to the bedroom and looked around. Saoirse's dresser was decorated with a few dozen baseball caps sporting patches from various military ships. I silently wondered how many of these ships had docked in *her* port.

Saoirse walked up behind me a few seconds later and wrapped her arms around my waist.

I turned around to face her. "Did you?" I raised my eyebrows towards the hats a few times. "With all of them?"

"Fuck noh! Not all of them!" she replied with eyes as big as golf balls.

"Some of them, yes. I like to have a good time, ya know. But I don't invite every military bloke I meet to my home or sleep with them either."

Saoirse motioned her arm towards the hats. "This is like my coin collection, ya see. But trust me, only a handful of these spunks cashed in with me." She kissed me on the cheek. "Now, do you want to eat breakfast in bed or at the table?"

"Table," I said.

She handed me a shirt and sweatpants and asked me to meet her downstairs.

I was pleasantly surprised by the breakfast spread that was laid out. Saoirse served me a traditional Australian breakfast and introduced me to Vegemite. She forewarned me I might not like the Vegemite. I admit, the name sounded suspect, and the black paste that resembled asphalt looked like someone had already eaten it. However, I was polite and tried it as part of my experiential learning... Let me just say that the air in my mouth tasted better than that hell on toast. It took two cups of coffee to get the rancid taste out of my mouth!

The rest of the breakfast was wonderful, though, and I complimented the cook with an empty plate.

Saoirse and I spent the rest of the day drinking Foster's Beer, eating barbeque, and playing cricket with Goodwin and her friend Addison in the backyard. It was the perfect day of no pretense. Saoirse never asked if I was married, and I didn't tell her. I knew I was never going to see her again and wanted the memory of our time together to be untainted. I could see light on the other side of misery for the first time in years.

After my tryst with Saoirse, I became a Tasmanian devil on a mission to find happiness and finally reclaim my balls. Chief was right. Women were throwing themselves at me left and right. I was the MVP of my personal World Series and was blowing backs out the park.

It was a world April wasn't a part of and knew absolutely nothing about. A world where I called the shots and got rewarded for being a man. No talks of money, no unrealistic expectations, and no shame. Pinch-hitting never felt so good.

But, as the saying goes, plans are great, but reality always has the last word. And right now my reality was screaming, "game over".

April was in the hospital, and I needed to fly home. The Chaplain called me into his office to give me the news. I hadn't phoned or accepted any calls from April in over three months, so she had her doctor contact the base in Australia. I was scheduled to fly out first thing in the morning and would return to Santa Barbara after my leave. I was pissed, but duty called.

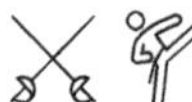

Time flies unless you're flying coach. And a twenty-one-hour flight was a long time to ruminate about a sick, cheating spouse. But Goodwin's words kept repeating in my head. "Just fuck, don't feel. Treat that barrack bunny snatch like an entertainment center and change the channel often and fondly."

It made sense, so I decided to use my flight time more wisely. I created movie reels in my head and entertained thoughts of all my recent conquests: the Aussie twin models who kept me naked for two days and had me exhausted for two weeks after. The volleyball player who spiked my balls and let me play in her sandbox. The court stenographer who taught me the art of dick-tation and communicating with my fingers. The fact that all I had to do was nod, smile, and keep my dick at attention. Yes, the playback reel of my sex inebriation was exactly what I needed to prep for the personal war awaiting me...

I landed in Buffalo around 9 am and went straight to my Mom's house. Mom was the only thing I'd missed since leaving Buffalo and the one constant I never had to second guess. Our initial reunion was short and sweet. We hugged, Mom cried, and I joked about the pathetic mongrels in my squad. The laughter and tears were good.

After devouring a plate Mom made of all my favorite foods, she drove me to the hospital to see April. The conversation on the ride there was casual and light. Mom didn't ask any questions about what was happening, but based on how she looked at me, she knew things between me and April weren't okay.

When I got to April's hospital room, a thin, straggly-haired male phlebotomist was sitting at the edge of her bed. He was drawing her blood to be tested for a transfusion. April's face lit up when she saw me, and she immediately started apologizing for her betrayal. It sounded performative, but she was extremely weak, so I did my best to console her. I told her our focus needed to be on her health, not our issues at the moment. She agreed and settled down.

The phlebotomist cleared his throat to get our attention. He told April he was done and would talk to her later. He stood there staring at April a little longer than necessary before turning to leave. The action seemed awkward and oddly personal. I brushed the feeling off as jet lag but caught a glimpse of his hospital badge before he left.

I continued to stay at my Mom's after April was released from the hospital a week later. I wasn't ready to share space with my public enemy. I'd done my best to emotionally disconnect from April's betrayal and didn't want to risk backsliding. Two days after she came home, we finally had the wake-up call we'd been hitting the snooze button on.

"You look cute today, Mylo. Is that a—"

I cut April off. I wasn't in the mood for pleasantries.

"April, I'm not here to play nice with you. So let's just rip the band-aid off, okay? Who was the guy who answered the phone when I called in the middle of the night?" I asked.

"Why wouldn't you answer my calls, Mylo? I called you for three months." April responded.

"Wow, you threw that like a rock," I scoffed and turned my head. "If you must know, Miss Money Hungry, you called after banking hours, and there was no more pending interest on my balls. And don't answer a question with a question. And... and stop trying to make me out to be the bad guy. You're the asshole dick licker in this situation. Shit, I'm out here serving and protecting your trifling ass while you're playing *Interview with a Vampire* with Chad, and his phlebotomist dick! How many shades of stupid do you think I am, April?" I looked her straight in the face.

She turned her head away. "He's no one Mylo. Just a friend who came over to sit with me because I wasn't feeling well. That's it. Really. You're reading too much—"

"A friend, huh?" I interrupted her. "Are you sure about that? Because Brenda and your mom gave me a different impression. Or maybe you haven't had time to get your stories straight between getting your blood work done." My words were clipped, but I remained calm.

"Mylo, it's obvious you've already made your mind up about this. Just tell me what you want me to say!" April was looking at me now. I could tell she was trying to flip the script, but I wasn't having it.

"Stop the bullshit, April. I didn't get sent home to be used for your amusement like some dancing bear. Either tell me the truth or leave me the fuck alone. This isn't a game."

I was waiting for April to strike back with her signature waterworks, but she didn't. She was lucid and unencumbered. "Okay, you want the truth? You really want the truth? Yeah, I'm fucking Chad, the phlebotomist, and he's more than just my friend, Mylo. He's the one who answered the phone because he's been staying here with me." April sighed. She looked relieved. But I knew her admission would come at a cost.

"Thank you for finally being honest with me, April. I wish you'd done it sooner. Makes me wonder..." I paused and walked behind the couch. My suspicious alertness was in overdrive.

"Let me ask you something. Are you in love with Chad?" April's expression didn't falter. Shit, she barely blinked. "Yes." April looked me in the eyes and gave a smug smirk for emphasis.

I pretended not to be phased."Okay, now we're getting somewhere." I continued.

"Let me ask you something else. What do I mean to you, April? Do you still love me?" I braced my hand on the back of the couch.

April stared me dead in the face and calmly said, "No, Mylo. I don't love you." It was the invalidation I needed to hear.

I walked over to April, gently tucked in the tag on her shirt collar, and whispered: "Your mattress tag was showing." Then I walked out.

For the first time, I realized April added NO value to our relationship. And although he looked like he needed a pint of blood and a good steak, I wasn't upset with Chad. I was embarrassed for myself. Ashamed that I'd been played by this sickly little trollop who'd consciously and deliberately gone out of her way to show me I wasn't enough.

I didn't deserve this shit. Goodwin was right; sometimes, being petty is the best solution.

Seeing a marriage counselor was April's idea. Claimed she wanted to attempt to save our relationship or whatever. I honestly no longer gave a fuck. The way I saw it, if the relationship started broken, it probably couldn't be fixed; optimism be damned. Besides, April's parents were footing the bill, so there was no need to argue.

April, let me pick the counselor. A tit for tat move, I'm pretty sure. I'd gotten a referral from her hematologist Dr. Cardozo since he and I had always been cool. When I'd visited April in the hospital on my leave home from Australia, Dr. Cardozo pulled me aside and asked: "Are you okay, Mylo? Is this too much for you? Do you feel depressed?"

So, I knew he understood my circumstance and would give me a great referral if I asked.

It was raining like crazy the day April, and I went to our counseling session. I remember joking that animals were going to start lining up two by two.

To make matters worse, the therapist's office was just as gloomy as the weather. The waiting area was painted in a sickly gray color that looked like years of regret and good intentions gone bad. I knew then that we were in the right place.

Dr. Ruffin wasn't at all what I'd expected. He was on the short side, ruddy-complected, mild-mannered, and about three years younger than Jesus. The only thing more noticeable than his age was his colossal nose. I'm pretty sure his sneezes could jump-start a car. Dr. Ruffin had this massive mahogany desk in the corner of his office with two boxes of Cheerios perched on top. I don't know why, but I immediately thought he was a vegetarian. I was too embarrassed to ask if my assumption was correct.

Once the session started, April took the reins. I admit, I was oddly surprised by her candor. Usually, she played things close to the vest, but today, she left the book wide open. She confessed to Dr. Ruffin that she was the reason why we were there. Told him about our age difference, me supporting her illness, the fact she'd cheated due to loneliness and boredom, and that her new lover lived with her while I served in the military. Hearing April say these things out loud to someone besides me made me feel grand and small at the same time. Again, confirmation we were in the right place.

When it was my turn to talk, I told Dr. Ruffin about April's refusal to move to Santa Barbara. I vented about her unrealistic financial expectations and relentless mockery of my military salary. I shared sending my whole check to April every month, keeping only $100 for myself. I confessed that April's "love you, too" never felt sincere and that she seemed addicted to provoking me. April stroked my arm while

I spoke, which annoyed the hell out of me. I moved my arm away from her several times before Dr. Ruffin asked her to stop. I could feel April simmering from the chastisement. I caught myself grinning.

Dr. Ruffin asked April how long her affair had been going on. April said it started immediately after I went to ops training. This meant she'd been fucking old boy since before we got married. I didn't tell Dr. Ruffin that this was new information for me, too. I'm sure my facial expressions spoke volumes. Dr. Ruffin nodded at April's response and asked if she loved the man she was having an affair with. April answered that she loved Chad, then added that she wasn't in love with me.

I stared at the boxes of Cheerios on Dr. Ruffin's desk and wondered if he ate them with soy milk.

What happened next surprised me. Dr. Ruffin sighed, removed his glasses, and leaned forward with a look of verdict on his face.

"Young lady, I know you have parents, but this needs to be said. April, you're a panderer and should be ashamed for all the hell you're putting this lad through. He's giving you unconditional support and all you're doing is taking advantage of his kindness and rubbing his nose in your self-absorption. Tell me, April, do you feel sorry for what you've done to Mylo?" Dr. Ruffin sat back calmly and folded his hands.

Without missing a beat, April broke into her classic fake crying. I gave her the side eye and shook my head. Dr. Ruffin looked back and forth between us, unphased.

After a few moments had passed, April took a dramatic pause and hiccupped, "I thought therapists weren't supposed to be judgmental! Why are you talking to me this way?" The crocodile tears were really flowing now. Dr. Ruffin shifted his weight in the chair.

"Well, April, I'm sure this isn't the first time you've been an exception to the rules. It seems you expect that. But you still haven't answered my question. Do you feel sorry for what you've done to Mylo?" Dr. Ruffin's composure remained stoic. I liked that he wasn't backing down and sank deeper into the couch cushion.

Instead of responding, April's crying got more hysterical, and she began showing signs of sickle cell crisis. The way things were looking, I was either gonna have to build an ark or call 911.

Either way, the session was fucked, and the situation needed some control. "Enough!" I yelled and stood up. "This is too much, and we've gotta stop before we have to bring an ambulance into this debacle! I'm taking April home!" I grabbed April by the arm and helped her to the car.

After this shit show, I was pretty sure my mind was the thing that was really in crisis. But as usual, it would have to wait.

Once April was settled, I returned to Dr. Ruffin's office to apologize. Dr. Ruffin looked me in the eye before handing me an appointment card with a time for two days later scribbled across it.

"Come back alone this time," he instructed, patting me on the shoulder. I nodded and went back to the car.

It was rush hour when we left Dr. Ruffin's office. April had calmed down and was staring a hole through me while we waited in traffic. You could cut the tension in the car with a hacksaw. I kept my eyes on the road and refused to give April any of my attention. I was still pissed about her performance at Dr. Ruffin's and didn't want to encourage more antics from her.

"Mylo," April put her hand on the steering wheel to get my attention. "I know I've said this before, but I'm truly sorry. There's no excuse for what I did to you." Her words broke some of the tension. "It was wrong of me, I admit it. But I get lonely and bored because I am always sick, so I have to find outlets for myself. And you know I'm not a needlepoint kinda girl."

When I didn't respond to her humor, April reached out and turned my chin to face her. "Listen, Mylo, I know being lonely and bored isn't an excuse either. I get that. Really I do. And I know what I've done has hurt you—A LOT. But you have to understand that at the end of the day, people need people." April moved her hand from my face and looked out the car window like nothing had happened.

I'm not sure how sincere her apology was, but April's words were the most important ones said to me: People. Need. People. I nodded to digest her words, then turned on the radio to kill the taste. It was a bitter ride home.

## Candy Girl

Illness can cause someone to lose their moral equilibrium. Drive them to overcompensate for their inability to control their body and foster a God-like superiority complex that overpowers and overwhelms everyone in their path. And sometimes, instead of using their powers for good, these sickly somebodies become the Boogeyman—that nefarious person with a van who lures kids with candy-coated promises and not-so-happy endings. I just wish someone had warned me that some Boogeymen wear pushup bras.

Visiting home was the thing I needed to tie my shoelaces together. Absence hadn't made my heart grow fonder, but it sure as hell was a palate cleanser for some much-needed clarity. For starters, I discovered April wasn't a likable person. And I'm not just saying this because she'd fucked me over. Her unlikability was innate and not just a character flaw. The prickly personality, Jekyll and Hyde mood swings, and masterful manipulation made April a bitch at a cellular level. I'd just been too inexperienced, and pussy whipped to see it. But now? Now it was plain as day—and the day wasn't looking too good. Distance is a powerful teacher.

There was no telling what kind of victim you were getting with April. Between crisis episodes from her sickness and fake Teflon tears that seemed to absolve her from accountability, April was the antihero who always got her way. But I couldn't wrap my brain around how she constantly managed to be surrounded by enablers. It was like the eighth wonder of the world. I mean, surely I wasn't the only one who didn't find her bitchiness endearing. But I guess when you come from a family of social darlings, you absorb the flavors of the pot you've been stewed in. Leave it to me to end up with a pot of mystery meat.

Then there were April's “”friends. Let's just say the people in April's life changed like the wind and were as interesting as warm glasses of milk. These weren't highbrow individuals. Quite the opposite, actually. I considered them opportunistic bottom feeders who existed slightly above any means necessary. And considering the amount of snobbery April prescribed to everything, her friend selection was pretty giggly. Nevertheless, these bottom feeders' presence (no matter how short-lived) seemed necessary for April's survival. I often wondered if lack of attention was a trigger for her disease crisis and lousy companion choices. Whatever the case, April's sickness made her thick-skinned to pain and immune to sensibility. It also gave her an obscure spotlight.

The way I see it, April's sickle cell disease was both a blessing and a curse. The identity associated with it gave her an exaggerated sense of entitlement to use people and a solid alibi to justify her actions. It also made maintaining friends and a sense of normalcy feel like running a marathon in ski boots, but April managed. Her obsessive self-interest made her resourceful enough to find a loophole that controlled both her disease AND her social life: prescription drugs. You see, the treatment for sickle cell symptoms in the United States is opioid painkillers. And while the treatment didn't make April a drug addict, it did make her an uninhibited pusher. Because when you're an attention whore like April, you don't subscribe to the realization that relationships aren't quid pro quo. Nope, instead, you socialize your disease treatment to score cool points and mask your insecurities: two birds, one pill.

Needless to say, anyone who came around April always got a pill or two (or three). But access to her candy store—like everything else with April—

came at a cost. Like a no shirt, no shoes policy, you were banned from her shop if you didn't play to April's impulses. So, like I said before, the lifespan of April's relationships was always short-lived. But a few exceptions managed to play the long game with April. Like Gia Mazza.

Gia was April's best friend and a force of nature. Gia grew up across the street from April and acted as the ying to her yang. They shared clothes, finished each other's sentences, and defended one another's choices. In essence, April and Gia were the perfect couple. And as dysfunctional as their thick and thin were, they were the most stable relationship in each other's lives.

Gia came from a fiery Italian family and didn't take shit from anyone—including April. To be honest, Gia was the only person I knew who could call April on her shit without giving a single fuck. Yeah, Gia was masterful. A scrappy little badass to be feared and admired. Hell, I wanted to be her when I grew up. So when I came home from Australia and learned that Gia and April were no longer friends, I looked for pigs to start flying.

The circumstances around April and Gia's breakup were sketchy as hell. April claimed she didn't know what caused Gia to kick her to the curb. And when I tried to probe, April turned on the tears, so I left that alone.

I was, however, able to get some lukewarm tea on the situation. For starters, Gia's family told April that Gia was behaving strangely and refusing to talk. Word on the street was that Gia was planning to get married, but her fiancé broke it off abruptly and moved to Washington, DC. Again, no one seemed to know the what or the why. The only things clear here were: (1) Gia had consecutively torched two relationships, and (2) she wasn't saying shit. The whole situation smelled like Swiss cheese to me. But my name was Bennett, and I wasn't in it. Shit, I was doing bad with April all by myself. I certainly didn't need Gia's misery or company added to the mix. So the mystery remained...

The next victim on April's exception list was this chick named Pearl. Apparently, Pearl got promoted to bestie when Gia exited left. They'd known each other for years, but I met Pearl for the first time during my visit home from Australia. I wasn't impressed. Pearl was a nice bag of eye candy but a strange bird and not the kind of odd duck April usually tethered herself to. And I do mean tethered.

Pearl was like April's shadow. And not in a protective friend kind of way. No, this was more of a jealous lover or needy high school girlfriend kinda cling. Depressed. Unsettling. Eeyore-ish. A lot like me when April and I first met.

The only difference was that the age gaps were reversed. You see, Pearl was more than a decade older than April. But evidently, ageism wasn't one of April's relationship filters.

However, pushing folks past their breaking point was definitely April's jam. And I was about to have a front-row seat to the swan song that ended April's jam session with Pearl.

April and I returned to the apartment from our session with Dr. Ruffin around 6 pm. We still hadn't spoken and were clueless that our silence was about to come to an involuntary end. We walked up the flight of stairs to our apartment and were greeted by Pearl standing at the top of the landing with a freshly shaved head and mascara streaking down her face. She looked like The Joker posing for Edvard Munch's painting *The Scream*. I silently wished I had some popcorn.

Pearl's new look put April in a different kind of crisis mode. "What the hell, Pearl! Why on earth did you do that to your hair!"

Pearl said she felt ugly and unloved and wanted a look to match.

April rolled her eyes and told Pearl to get her shit together because pathetic wasn't a good look.

From there, the argument grew into what appeared to be more of a lover's quarrel than a catfight. I watched the drama unfold like a peeping Tom, thankful the trouble wasn't mine.

"Look here, you spoiled little bitch." Pearl seethed. "You've got a lot of nerve telling me to get my shit together." Pearl's fists were balled, and beads of sweat pooled where her hair used to be. "Got me out here looking like Uncle Fester on crack. And for what? It's not like I'm getting anything out of this. All you do is use people, April. Like your husband here, who foots the bill for this apartment, and you entertaining any damn body who compliments your slutty ass. *You're* the one who ain't shit." Pearl dragged her hands across her head and then wiped them on her jeans.

"Look at you, April. Knees all ashy. You probably have whiplash from all that oral gratification you give out. Say ahhhh!" Pearl opened her mouth wide and got in April's face. "But *I'm* the one who's out of order. Pshaw!" Pearl put her hands on her hips in a Superman pose. "Speaking of out of order, what about that mop-headed dipshit Chad? Has hubby met that loser yet?" April stood shell-shocked, but the Pearl Harbor attack was far from over.

"You're a real piece of work, ya know. I'm sure hubby didn't know that while he's been off being all he could be, your panties were easier to get into than a community college. I wouldn't feel bad if this young man finally said to hell with your ungrateful hoe ass and left you! Your sickly little ass ain't worth two cents in Chinese money!" Pearl paused, sniffed towards April then turned towards me.

"Listen, here, honey." She crooned calmly. "You're a good man and way too classy for this slut muffin over here. You're young, fine as hell, and got a lot going for you. Don't let someone like her hold you back." Pearl pointed at April with her back turned to her. "Do yourself a huge favor, Mylo, and level up while you've got the chance. Cause trust me, her juice ain't worth the squeeze."

April had finally had enough and got nose-to-nose with Pearl. "Get the hell out of here, Pearl! I mean it! NOW!!" she grunted through clenched teeth.

"Is that the best you've got, Oral-B?" Pearl let out a sinister laugh. "It's too late, you lame-ass bitch." Pearl pushed a finger into April's forehead and stepped back. "I've already grabbed my stuff from your place. So please know I won't be coming back here, EVER." Pearl turned and picked up a box sitting next to the door. "My daughter will be here in a few minutes to pick me up. I'll wait for her outside." Pearl threw a key chain across the landing, then flipped April the bird as she walked down the steps.

April immediately launched into a crying fit and crumpled into a ball on the floor. I ignored her performance and followed Pearl downstairs. When I caught up to her on the sidewalk, we both smiled. I'd misjudged Pearl and gave her a high five. I whistled the Seven Dwarfs Heigh-Ho song while we waited for her daughter to arrive. Nothing else needed to be said.

Once Pearl's daughter arrived, I helped her put the box in the car and watched the headlights disappear. I contemplated getting in my own car and leaving but went against my better judgment. Instead, I went back upstairs to check on April. I was still whistling the Heigh-Ho song when I walked into the apartment.

## Girl to the Third Power

Trouble comes in threes. I'm not certain why. I guess the universe's sick sense of humor reminds us that third times aren't always the charm. Threes. Its trouble sounds like a Chris Rock comedy bit: raw, unapologetic, with impeccable timing and an offbeat delivery. *"Haha, motherfucker! Here's a trifecta of misfortune for thinking you knew better. You're welcome, dummy!"* Threes. When threes happen, the joke's always on someone.

April's track record in the friend zone was currently 0-2. This third strike was going to be a game-changer. Blurred lines, no boundaries.

When I returned to the apartment, April was on the phone with Gia's sister, Noemi. April and Noemi were having a catty conversation about the Pearl Harbor bombing that just went down. I shook my head and let the television watch me while they gossiped. Between our disastrous therapy session with Dr. Ruffin and the sneak attack from Pearl that followed, I was so tired I could spit.

I wasn't paying attention to the show that was on, but somewhere between commercials for Grey Poupon and Ms. Cleo's psychic readings, I heard April invite Noemi over. I didn't think anything of it. I was too focused on watching the back of my eyelids. That was a BIG mistake.

Noemi was gunning to be the kill shot in my and April's relationship. Her claim to fame was being a serial addict who didn't meet a drug, bottle of booze, or orifice she didn't want to fuck. She's also the only person I've ever known to get a DUI in a cul-de-sac. I always thought that Noemi hung around April when she wanted to get her life right and a good meal. Now I understand that it was an aiding and abetting kind of relationship that took place when someone passed the peas.

Oddly enough, Noemi and April's friendship was the only one that made perfect sense to me. Instead of yin and yang, they had disease, insecurity, and control issues as bonding agents. And because of their chronic illnesses, Noemi and April were the homecoming queens of bouncing back from rock bottom. So, it seemed natural for April to call Noemi when the bottom fell out of her relationship with Pearl.

I don't remember falling asleep, but I do remember feeling something being pushed in my mouth. The sensation jarred me enough to jerk my head and jump out of the chair. I immediately rubbed my throat. It felt like I'd swallowed something.

April was standing in front of me, holding a soda. "Here, take a sip."

"Did you put a pill in my mouth, April?"

"Don't worry about it, Mylo. We had a lot of drama today, and you need something to help you relax."

"But I was already sleeping..."

She gave me the same combination smile-frown that her mother always wore and moved the soda can closer to my lips.

My eye twitched. I drank the soda but was puzzled.

About 20 minutes later, I was a zombie. I have no clue how much time passed after that. All I know is that I woke up feeling like I was sleepwalking with activities. But I was in bed. The room was dim, and the big red numbers on the alarm clock made me think my eyes were bleeding. Somehow, I knew it wasn't the end of the world, but I thought I could see it from the edge of the nightstand.

Suddenly, I felt touching and heard voices. Both female. I looked past the covers and saw April and Noemi. They were both naked and taking turns performing oral on me. Being the freak that I am, this should have been my Mount Rushmore moment. But my dumb ass got paranoid and jumped instead. Whatever this was, it didn't feel right. April straddled me and told me to relax. Then she dragged her finger down the middle of my chest and said she wanted to do this for me. I tried to respond but couldn't get my lips to move. There were clouds on the ceiling, and the room was foggy. What the hell was in that pill April gave me?

April and Noemi began making out with each other before taking turns on me. I kept seeing fog, too blitzed to enjoy the ride. I swear I heard Chris Rock laughing in my left ear.

When I finally regained my faculties, it was light outside, and the world felt black. I just wanted to shower and watch a cartoon. I looked to my left, and Noemi was lying beside me in bed. Her breasts were exposed, and she was fingering herself. I didn't see April anywhere. I grabbed the sheet and scurried out of bed.

When I finished showering, Noemi was gone, and April was making pancakes with bananas and lots of butter, just like I liked them. I sat down at the table and stared at the placemat. I needed something besides the awkwardness in the room to focus on. April brought my plate over and sat down. The food was a welcomed diversion from her stare. I was reaching for Mrs. Butterworth's waist when April grabbed my hand.

"Mylo, about last night" April began.

I moved my hand away from her and started pouring the syrup.

April sighed and scooted back in her chair. "Well, I... I just... Mylo, I wanted to do something special for you. After everything that happened yesterday and what's been happening while you've been deployed..." April paused and got up to stand behind the chair. "Mylo, what I'm trying to say is what I did with Chad was wrong. I know I said that in the car yesterday, but it didn't seem like enough. So I gave you the night with me and Noemi to try and call a truce."

I put down the syrup and finally looked at April. I wanted to see if she was being serious. Unfortunately, she was. I pushed my plate to the side and tented my hands on the table in front of me. April inched to the other side of her chair.

"So let me understand." I leaned forward and paused. "You think a double order of pussy and some pancakes is a consolation prize for cheating on me. Is that what you're saying, April? An eye for a clit?"

April fiddled with the drawstring of her sweatpants. Something about her silence made my backbone snap into place.

"Let's get a few things straight. First of all, April, you and I aren't fighting. We're trying to fix a marriage you broke, and we both agreed to repair it. So the fact that you think we need a truce says a lot. But that's not even the part that hurts. What's really fucked up is that you had to drug me to fuck me over again because the words I'm sorry weren't good enough. Does that sound special to you?" I'd leaned forward so hard my elbows rested on top of the pancakes.

April looked horrified. Mrs. Butterworth was grinning at me.

"I can't believe I sacrificed happily ever after for some psychosexual pill pusher with a medical alert button and Metamucil on her breath. But here we are. So let me make this easy for you. I forgive you, April. There! Is that what you wanted? Or do you need drugs and my dick up your ass for it to mean something? Don't get it twisted, April. I'm not calling you a hoe, but it's obvious you know some people. Pearl certainly had you pegged."

April started crying and ran into the bedroom. I grabbed my wallet and keys and left. It was April's third strike, and I was out.

## Godfather

The problem with being conflict averse is that you wind up working as a team with the voices in your head. And mine were annoyingly passive-aggressive. "I hate being with you. I'll be back tomorrow. You can be anything you want to be. Why do you want to do that?" If only the voices in my head could be seen and not heard. But unfortunately, my passive-aggressive filter didn't register that high. So, for now, there was a full-blown war zone going on in my head about my shitty situationship with April. One side of my brain was pissed she'd played me like a numbers racket. The other side was apologizing for getting upset about it. I kept replaying something Cedric used to say: "*Man, if you have to worry about a woman, she's not worth worrying about.*" Jesus, I wish I'd understood what that meant before I'd met April. Now I was stuck between a rock and a marriage license, settling for failed resolutions.

When I returned to Dr. Ruffin's office, the boxes of Cheerios were still on his desk. I thought maybe I'd have the courage to ask him about being a vegetarian. I sat staring at his nose and contemplated how much it would be worth full of nickels. See, this is why I dislike being alone with my thoughts. They're always out of bounds. Doc was going to make a fortune off of me.

I was all out of sorts because seeing a shrink isn't like visiting a regular doctor. I mean, it's not like you can point to your boo-boo and say this is where it hurts. Life would be simpler if they made Band-Aids for your conscience. But I don't think Costco makes economy sizes that large.

So, since I didn't know what to say, I kept calculating how many nickels would fit in each of Dr. Ruffin's nostrils. But calculations weren't my thing, so my mind switched to imagining if his glasses would stay in place if his ears were missing.

Dr. Ruffin either read my thoughts or felt guilty charging me for dead air and broke the silence. "Do you know why I asked you to return here today, Mylo?" Dr. Ruffin asked.

"I don't know, Doc. Maybe you want to ask why an old soul like me was attracted to a mid-life crisis before reaching my twenties."

Dr. Ruffin chuckled a bit. "Well, no, but I'd be interested in hearing your response to that."

"I'm not sure I have one, Doc. I just figured that's what I'd want to know if I was sitting in your seat." I paused for a moment. "Is it okay if I ask you a question?"

"Sure, I'm okay with that, Mylo. What would you like to ask?"

"Are you a religious man, Doc?"

"That's an interesting question, Mylo. May I ask why you want to know?"

"Well, being a shrink is a lot like being a priest. You know confessionals, confidentiality, no judgment, the whole nine. So I'm wondering, is therapy your religion, or do you answer to a higher power?"

Dr. Ruffin was silent momentarily and then responded, "Before I answer that, Mylo, may I ask if you're religious?"

"Yes sir, I am. My father's a Baptist minister, so I'm religious by default. The Lord is my shepherd; I shall not want is coded into my DNA."

"I see," Dr. Ruffin acknowledged.

"One last question, and then I promise I'll answer yours." He paused. "Are you staying married to April because of your religious upbringing?"

I just stared at Dr. Ruffin, uncertain of how to respond.

"Okay, Mylo. I'll let you chew on that last question while I answer yours." Dr. Ruffin removed his glasses and leaned back in his chair. "Well, I'm not religious, nor do I consider therapy a substitute for religion. I actually have a very jaded view of religion." Dr. Ruffin coughed and repositioned himself in the chair.

"To me, religion is like organized crime. Jesus saves, but God kills every second of every day. It's a calculated power play. Religion shows up as both the villain and the hero to keep people from questioning their oppression. Crime lords and godfathers. They're the equalizers we believe exist to save us from ourselves. And to your point, one could argue that therapy is a mob-like racket. I mean, shrinks do claim to use their powers for good while taking your money. We also know where the bodies are buried, but don't force anyone to swim with the fishes. It's a slight difference in perspective, just like everything in life." Dr. Ruffin folded his hands and crossed his ankles.

"But to be truthful, Mylo, I can't tell you who's right and who's wrong. You study psychology long enough, and you can find the justification for just about anything. Trust me, it often keeps me up at night. But my job is to help you see and accept yourself for who you are so you can live without apology." Dr. Ruffin reached for his glasses and put them back on.

"We can't control the circumstances we're born into, Mylo. But we can control how we allow them to impact us. You're your own moral majority."

We both remained silent for a few beats to let the logic settle. It was ocean-deep.

"Wow. I don't know whether I should pass a collection plate or hit you in the knee with a tire iron." I raised my head to the ceiling and performed the sign of the cross. "All jokes aside, Doc, thank you for sharing your views with me. I've never heard anyone draw those parallels before." I grabbed the gray throw pillow next to me and held it on my lap."You've got a pretty awesome pulpit for an agnostic."

Dr. Ruffin grinned and pushed his glasses up the bridge of his nose. I fought the urge to call him Nostrildamus.

"Thank you, Mylo. You're pretty wise beyond your years for a Baptist. So, I guess that makes us equals. Tell me, Mylo, as a religious man, what do you want your redemption story with April to be? Do you want to be the martyr?"

"Dang. You cut right to the chase, Doc. Guess you need to make these minutes count." I pulled at the zipper on the throw pillow, trying to formulate my thoughts. "I honestly don't know. I mean, maybe I do have a savior complex. I'm a real sucker for a damsel in distress. Look who I married." I was eyeing a discoloration on the carpet, struggling to determine if it was a dead bug.

"I haven't thought about this before. But I do know that I don't want to be a cliché or statistic like my mom and dad. They divorced when I was little because my preacher dad was a drunk and a cheat. So, I guess I don't want that history repeating itself. Do I deserve better than April? I don't know. Do I wonder what my life would be like now if I'd never met April? Have I ever imagined what would've happened if I'd pumped the breaks early in the relationship to see if she was worth the long game? Absolutely times 10. Listen, I know I fell in love way too fast and let sex dictate the relationship. I don't know what my problem was."

I moved from the couch and walked over to the boxes of Cheerios. Reading the label felt like an appropriate thing to do.

"Shit, I wish I would have listened to everyone who warned me not to get involved with April. Not just listened but *acted*. But now I feel stuck. Like I'll never find anyone else like April." I put the cereal box down and sat on the edge of Dr. Ruffin's desk.

"You know, my girlfriend before April used to tell me I'd never find anyone who'd treat me like her. And she treated me like dog shit. Her words haunt me... It's like I enjoy abuse. Like life isn't okay for me unless I feel I can't do any better. So, the way I see it, it's cheaper to keep her, right? I mean, April has an expiration date, after all. Isn't that the silver lining in all of this? The redemption song? No woman, no cry. I don't know if that makes me Jesus, Bob Marley, or Don Corleone in this story."

"None of the above, Mylo. It makes you human," Dr. Ruffin responded. "You're simply doing what seems right to you. But tell me, Mylo, why do you keep hanging on to the asterisk that you're the only person who can care for April?"

"I don't know. Is it too early to send her to Shady Pines?" I asked. The remark was sarcastic, but a part of me was serious.

"What would you say if I told you I could help you get out of your marriage to April?"

"I'd say it sounds like something that hurts."

"I can understand why you'd feel that way, Mylo. Your experience with divorce isn't something you want to relive." Dr. Ruffin stopped and took a deep sigh.

"You know, Mylo, sometimes the pursuit of happiness is the *cause* of our unhappiness."

I looked at Doc like his nose had shrunk.

"Let me explain." Dr. Ruffin continued. "It's like the saying the gold in the garbage. You were hoping April was going to be this magical treasure that had been buried in all the relationship garbage you'd experienced. But when you figured out she was just shinier garbage, you felt embarrassed, unfulfilled, and stuck. You need to realize that mistakes are nothing more than something to get used to. They're meant to help us learn, move on, and do better for ourselves." Dr. Ruffin removed his glasses again and gripped the armrests.

"Earlier, you referred to yourself as an old soul. I'm guessing you feel like you've had to be older than your years to survive. But I want to challenge you to stop leveling down to feel grown up. Despite what you've been taught, Mylo, being happy is not selfish or a sin. You've already gone against other people's opinions to explore happiness with April. But based on what I've heard, happiness never happened with her. Mylo, I'm saying that you don't have to let April stop you from digging for gold. Find a new space to dig without her. Get your happiness. Because April's already started to dig without you."

Doc had read me like a cheap romance novel. And I'm not gonna lie, the truth stung. A LOT. He was right. I needed to level up.

But Doc didn't understand what I was up against with April AND her family. This whole mess was a big, ugly family affair from start to finish. And despite all his experience and good intentions, I wasn't convinced Doc had enough muscle to help me battle April before she took her impending dirt nap. I already knew the Barnes family wouldn't play nice or easily concede to a peon like me. Especially if it didn't happen on THEIR terms. The way I saw it, I had a better chance of walking to Mars by Monday than breaking ties with the Barnes. They'd drag me (and the court system) to hell and back before letting that happen. But I didn't tell Doc any of this. I also didn't tell him I'd been digging in the garbage while in the Air Force. I liked Doc and all, but my hoe phase was classified information.

So, I let him do his counseling thing without revealing that my mind was made up. For the rest of the session, I listened, responded, and wondered: of all the cereals out there, why would a vegetarian choose Cheerios?

I learned a lot talking with Dr. Ruffin that day. His questions and insights challenged me in a way that made me feel seen, heard, and smart. Before that, I don't think I'd ever experienced those three things simultaneously or at all. I was surprised by how much I liked it and the radical acceptance that came with it.

I realized I was coping in a no-win situation and trying to survive it with as little conflict as possible. It wasn't the greatest war strategy, but it didn't suck, either. I had the military to return to, my secret infidelity to play with, and a wife with a biological clock that was almost out of minutes. That was my end game. I just had to bide my time. And that's exactly what I did.

*********************************************************************************

# Reckoning
## Hard Truths Cut Both Ways

# No Bones About It

I wasn't a big fan of the name Bones at first. Probably because I was always the 98-pound weakling growing up. My mom *still* refers to me as skin and bones, even though I now have a dad bod and love handles. And most of the women I've dated over the years have described me as a fixer-upper. In case you're wondering, having great bones isn't a compliment outside of the housing market. Oh, and I've never seen the TV show Bones. Hey, what can I say? Emily Deschanel doesn't do it for me.

But skeletons in the closet don't scare you when you produce a true crime podcast for a living. They make your messes acceptable or (at the very least) give you a support group to cope. Choose your poison.

In some ways, bones are the shell companies that launder our secrets and provide alibis for our unsettled indiscretions. That is until something comes along and raids your closet. So, despite triggering my inferiority complexes (yes, I have multiple), the Bones alias has started to grow on me. Anything's better than a pandemic and the fact that I haven't boned a woman in months. That's another strike against the name. Guess that fan club will have to wait.

By the way, my real name is Darius Rudland. I grew up in Buffalo, where I developed commitment issues, a love for beef on weck, and a soft spot for difficult women. But I wasn't always that way. Before I moved to Washington, D.C., and started producing podcasts about malice and murder, I was all about settling down, white picket fences, hearts, rainbows, happily ever after—the whole nine yards. But life happened. Now I'm a 53-year-old confirmed bachelor living in the basement of a couple's house I found on Craigslist. No, I'm not broke. I'm just broken and like to keep a low profile, which is pretty easy to do during a pandemic.

Hitting snooze on the coming and going of everything has been both cathartic and terrifying for me. For one, having nothing but time and opportunity to watch Netflix has drastically lowered my risks of fucking up. And you won't believe what internet porn has done for my relationship angst. In the immortal words of Olivia Pope, "It's handled". But the scary bit is the nostalgia we've all been nesting in. Salvaging the sense that not all good things in life are gone. Makes you wonder if hell and hope can coexist. But I'm a pessimist who thinks the dildo of life rarely shows up lubed. Yet despite all my mental posturing, nostalgia was the one thing that completely rattled my bones.

The past is a tricky thing. It can summon times when life felt safe, and you didn't know better or leave you feeling stuck. I don't revisit the past because of the latter. I'm stuck-averse. It's why I don't do relationships and am permanently unattached.

But I saw a scene on TV today that unearthed a skeleton I'd hoped to keep buried. A man and a woman were chatting in a diner, and the woman tucked a piece of hair behind the man's ear. It was nothing major. The gesture was quick and very subtle. But the memories it conjured up... Let's just say skeletons with soft edges often leave the deepest wounds.

I met my skeleton with soft edges at a diner in 1992. I needed a quiet place to read and a cheap meal, so it was my two-for-one special. I was sitting at the counter highlighting passages in a book for a war reporting assignment when I felt someone plop down on the stool next to me. I saw a mound of long black curls from the corner of my eye and kept reading.

A few seconds later, the mound of curls tapped me on the elbow and asked for one of my fries. I put my book down and faced her. Then, without blinking, Curly Girl grabbed a handful of fries from my plate and shoved them in her mouth.

"You ever notice how food tastes better from someone else's plate?" Curly Girl asked, chewing with her mouth open.

"You're welcome." I shoved my plate of fries in front of her and continued reading. She was cute, but I needed to focus on finishing my book.

"What, are you a broke college student or something?" Curly Girl interrupted.

"How'd you guess?" I kept reading, hoping she'd get the hint. She leaned across the counter and swept her finger behind my ear.

"See, still wet behind the ears." She held up her finger and grinned.

Her touch made me gulp. It wasn't meant to be sexual, but nonchalance never felt so good.

I focused back on my book so she couldn't see I was flushed.

"I tried college once. It didn't take," Curly Girl declared.

"What happened?" I asked, still reading.

"I'm an Aries, and I like to fight." She shoved another french fry in her mouth and kept her mouth closed this time.

"Well, lucky for me, I didn't resist giving you my fries." I went back to reading.

Curly Girl grabbed the book off the counter and turned it over.

"You're reading about Vietnam. Interesting. You ever been there?"

"Yep." I lied. "What about you?"

"Nope. I'm just being nosy. Hey, do they really eat dogs over there?"

"Yeah, they do." I recovered the book from her and looked for my highlighter.

"I'm curious," Curly Girl continued.

"Is there a difference in taste between a rottweiler and a cocker spaniel? Or do all dogs taste like chicken?" Curly Girl was straight-faced.

I put the highlighter down and looked her straight in the eyes. I watched her forehead crinkle before she broke out laughing. She sounded like an asthmatic cat which made me belly laugh.

"Now I've got your attention, Mr. Bookworm. Hi, I'm Gia Mazza." Gia wiped her hand on her jeans before extending it.

"What, no brass knuckles?" I joked, then shook her hand.

"Nice to finally know the name of the person who bogarted my fries. I'm Darius Rudland."

Gia shrugged and ate another french fry. She'd stolen my fries and my heart.

The months ahead with Gia were my favorite mistakes. She was loud and fiery and alive. Her brashness and my quiet confidence were the perfect compliments. Where I edited, she had no filter. Being with her tasted like freedom, I thought I'd found my missing piece. But the journey to completion is often flawed. And my relationship with Gia was full of potholes.

The potholes weren't bad for the most part. But there was a big one that completely derailed our togetherness: jealousy. Now, the jealousy didn't come from us or our exes. It came from Gia's best friend, Mimi.

Gia and Mimi grew up across the street from one another and were basically Siamese twins—even as adults. However, their friendship wasn't equal. Mimi had a chronic illness, and Gia spent a lot of time looking after her. And if I'm being completely candid, their relationship towed a fine line between platonic and romantic. It was a curiously complex friendship, to say the least.

I always had the feeling that Mimi didn't care much for me. She didn't say or do anything to give that impression. I take that back. Mimi made me feel like I was in the way. Like I was a third wheel that needed to give Gia space. It was silent and unsettling, but I took it on the chin in the name of love, serenity, and not appearing crazy.

At first, I thought Mimi's sullenness towards me was a side effect of my honeymoon phase with Gia. Initially, Gia and I abandoned the world for french fries, french kisses, and each other, so Mimi's abandonment issues were justified. But our relationship was fully integrated into reality now, and it was clear that Mimi's issue with me wasn't just a phase. It was a battle to control Gia's heart.

The first signs of Mimi's jealousy materialized on our first double date. Gia told Mimi that we were spending the day at Goat Island. Mimi invited herself and her boyfriend, Chad, to tag along. I didn't mind, and the day with them was pleasant enough. We walked, explored, and listened to nature. The tensions were low, and the laughter was high. Having Chad as a fourth wheel and buffer between the Siamese twins was nice. And based on the day's events, I was ready to exhale my uncertainties about Mimi.

We drove Mimi and Chad back to their apartment at the end of the date. We all got out of the car and did the polite "It was so nice getting together" and "let's do it again real soon."

Then Mimi pulled me over to the side of the car. She told me how happy she was that Gia found a nice guy like me and to make sure I treated Gia right. I let Mimi know that my love and intentions for Gia were honorable and pure. Mimi hugged me and as she was letting go, she whispered in my ear, "I was the only love in Gia's life until you came along." She looked at me with a quick sneer that gave me chills. Then she smiled, turned, and said goodbye to Gia.

From there, Mimi's cock blocking got more assertive. Incessant phone calls, fake medical emergencies, and dramatic crying spells that went on for hours if things didn't go according to Mimi's agenda. It was EXHAUSTING. But Gia was a trooper and didn't stop putting Mimi in her place. Despite Mimi's efforts to spoil our relationship, seeing how Gia balanced her care and concern for both of us made me love her even more.

After almost a year of dating, I asked Gia to marry me. It was a modest proposal at the diner where it all started. I ordered Gia a plate of french fries and had the waitress serve them with the ring box on top. Gia said "yes" immediately and asked the waitress to bring her another plate of fries.

We toasted our engagement with milkshakes, then drove to her parents' house to tell them the news. Gia's mom and dad were ecstatic, and before we knew it, her siblings and their families were there to congratulate us.

Gia called Mimi and asked her to come over. When Mimi arrived, Gia opened the door and flashed her ring. "I'm getting married!" Gia squealed.

Mimi walked through the door and didn't say a word. Gia stood grinning at Mimi with her hand up in the air, wiggling her fingers. Mimi lunged forward and shoved Gia.

"How could you do this to me, Gia? You can't get married! You haven't known him that long! What the hell are you doing?" Mimi was screaming, and the entire house went still.

"Mimi, calm down. I thought you'd be happy for me like I've always been for you." Gia's voice was composed, but her fists were clenched.

Mimi looked around the room and saw everyone staring at her. She burst into tears and ran out the back door.

Gia walked out behind her. I saw them through the window, sitting on the swing set in the backyard. I continued mingling and kept a close watch outside.

After about 20 minutes, Gia came back inside alone. She told me Mimi left but wanted to extend her congratulations to me. I knew Gia was lying. I kissed her on the forehead and hugged her. I realized then that marriage would be the most complicated group project ever.

## Sock It to Me

A week after the engagement announcement I got a call from Mimi. She'd been out of dodge since her dramatic exit and sounded surprisingly chipper. I informed her that Gia wasn't around and offered to take a message. Mimi said it was fine and that she wanted to talk to me. Warning bells immediately went off.

The call was brief. Mimi apologized for making a scene at our engagement announcement and congratulated me for making her best friend the happiest girl alive. Her apology sounded saccharin and forced. I thanked her and expressed how elated I was to marry someone as special as Gia.

"Well, remember, I knew her first," Mimi snapped.

"Excuse me?" I interjected.

"I'm just yanking your chain, Darius. Geez, lighten up!" Mimi huffed.

"Anyway, I'd like to host a get-together for you and Gia tonight. You know, to apologize and properly congratulate you on the engagement. Can you be here around 7? Oh, and please don't tell Gia. I want to surprise her. And make sure you arrive separately. I'm planning something special for her; if you come together, it'll spoil it."

"Sure, I'll be there at 7, and I promise not to spoil the surprise. Should I bring anything?" I asked.

"No, dear, just bring yourself. I'll take care of everything," she chirped. "Okay, love, I've got lots to do. See you at 7. And don't mention anything to Gia. I'll make sure she gets here when she's supposed to." Mimi hung up before I could say goodbye.

I have this quirky habit of obsessing over random items when I want to avoid something. I'm pretty easygoing, so it doesn't happen often. But I remember obsessing like nobody's business on this particular day.

After I hung up the phone with Mimi, I couldn't stop thinking about socks. Yes, socks. I was trying to decide how much patience I'd have in picking out socks to wear to Mimi's soiree. Should I wear dress socks, ankle socks, no socks, themed socks, patterned socks, plain socks... I felt like I was in a Dr. Seuss parody. The last time I deliberated this long over a piece of clothing was at my grandfather's funeral. On that day, it was neckties.

I went to my sock drawer and started sorting through it. Every pair of socks I fished out had a hole. Some noticeable, some not, but holes, nonetheless. After surveying a third of my sock drawer, I finally found a pair with a skull and crossbones and no holes. I'd worn them with a Halloween costume a few years before, and now they'd resurfaced. I was relieved. But the irony of unholy socks with skulls should have been a warning. A benevolent sign from the universe that the death of my future with Gia was imminent.

I arrived at Mimi's apartment at 7:03 pm. I hadn't planned on parking issues and prayed Mimi wouldn't berate me for being three minutes late. I was relieved when Gia's sister, Noemi, answered the door. Noemi invited me in and told me to have a seat, Mimi was in the bedroom. I asked Noemi where everyone was. She said she didn't know and excused herself to help Mimi.

A few minutes later, Noemi and Mimi came out of hiding. Mimi grabbed a platter of cheese and crackers and placed them on the coffee table in front of me.

"Nice socks," she snarked and curled her lip.

I nodded and smiled. It was too early in the evening for antagonism.

"So, where's Chad?" I asked Mimi.

"Oh, Chad had to work late. He'll be here later." Mimi responded.

"Gotcha. So, who else is coming?" I was trying to make small talk, but Mimi seemed annoyed.

"Don't worry about that, Darius." She went into the kitchen and brought out a glass of wine. "Here, drink this. You need to relax."

I took the glass from her and had a few sips. I could tell I needed all the liquid courage I could muster to survive the evening, so I finished the glass.

That was a mistake. A few minutes later, I started feeling extremely drowsy. My tongue felt like it was five inches thick, and I couldn't talk. I slid lower and lower on the couch—then the room went black.

I woke up feeling like a wishbone. My hands were tied to something, and Noemi was between my legs doing unspeakable things not suitable for a future in-law. It was like I'd clicked my heels three times and moved in with a hallucination. When Noemi noticed I was awake, she slithered up my torso and bit the cleft on my chin. Her hair smelled like the back of a belt strap. I felt myself gag. Then I felt someone untying me. Her hair was in two long pigtails. She looked like a naughty Pocahontas. Pocahontas was kissing me and licking my neck as she untied my hands. It was Mimi. I tried to yell, but no sound came out. Mimi put her finger over my mouth and straddled me. Then she started to laugh. Once I was untied, there were so many hands and legs everywhere that I'm pretty sure Hindus were somewhere praying to us. All I knew was that I was supposed to be celebrating my engagement holding a champagne flute, not my future sister-in-law's ass.

I don't know when it started, but there was yelling. Lots of yelling. I was alone on the bed and there were people in the room yelling. One of them was Gia. The sight of her sobered me, and I finally sat up. It was at that point that I realized I was butt naked. I didn't know where my clothes were, so I took off one of my skull socks and put it on over my penis. Guess I'm modest even when I'm high. The yelling continued...

"Shut the hell up, Noemi! I already know that the meter's running when you're on your back. So just take whatever money's in my purse and leave!" Gia ran a hand through her curls and cursed when it snagged in her engagement ring.

"Dammit to hell! I anticipated an engagement dinner and an apology, not watching my fiancé get blown by my best friend and sister. I'd expect something like this from Noemi. But you, Mimi? You?" Gia stood in front of Mimi, exasperated.

Mimi twisted the ends of her pigtails and looked at the floor.

"I knew you were selfish and petty, but this is next level, Mimi. I've seen you do some dirty, slimy, underhanded shit, but THIS? How long have you been planning this, huh? What, Darius didn't follow the script in that fucked up head of yours, so this was plan B? And adding my sister? That was a masterful cherry on top. Remember, as kids, you used to lick all your favorite cookies so no one else would eat them? I guess this is your grown-up version with cock instead of snacks." Gia let out a sinister snicker and leaned against the dresser.

"I NEVER imagined in a thousand lifetimes you'd be capable of doing something this low and DISGUSTING to ME! ME Mimi! Me, who's always taken care of you, defended you, covered for you! But when I get some happiness for myself—some REAL happiness—this is how you decide to treat me. You drugged my fiancé and slept with him!!!" Gia was in tears.

Mimi tried to console her, but Gia hauled off and slapped her.

I saw my pants folded on a chair next to the bed and grabbed them. I thought it was a good time to get up. "I'm gonna go get a snack." I heard myself say. Nobody seemed to notice, so I went to the kitchen while the yelling continued.

"But you don't understand, Gia!" Mimi pleaded. "I'm your soulmate, not him. You need to spend your life with me. I've only got a few years left to live, and I want to spend them with you. I want to spend the rest of my life with you, Gia!"

Gia stormed out of the room. Mimi followed on her heels.

"Listen to me, Gia. LISTEN!" Mimi screamed. Gia stopped but kept her back to Mimi while she continued her plea.

"Gia, when I'm gone, you'll still have time to have the life you want. You'll still be young enough. And... and I'm fine with you having kids with someone else. Just as long as we can be a family together. You're my family, Gia! YOU'RE. MY. FAMILY." Mimi stopped talking and leaned against a chair.

Gia stood in place, breathing heavily. She rubbed her forehead before turning around. Then she started clapping. "Bravo, Mimi! Bra-vo! That was your best performance yet. Whew! I don't know how you pulled it off with no tears. I think that's a first for you. Maybe it's the Pocahontas braids. Yeah, that's it. And the Academy Award goes to..." Gia pounded her hands on the dining table as a drum roll. "Mimi Barnes for her portrayal of the Indian slut, *Hypnotized by Dick*!" Gia breathed into her hands to make crowd noises, then sat down.

"You can stop with the woe-as-me manipulations, Mimi. I've experienced too many of them, and you've gone too far this time. Do you honestly believe I'd want to build a life with you after what you pulled tonight? Your sickle cell disease must have really fucked up your logic." Gia got up and moved over to where Mimi was standing.

"Mimi, being your friend has been an endless, pointless chore, and I'm done with you." Gia hacked and spit in Mimi's face.

I came out of the kitchen as Gia was leaving. Her eyes were bloodshot, her chest was heaving, and all I wanted was to push the curls away from her face.

Gia stopped for a moment and looked at me. I was holding a piece of bread with my pants slung over my shoulder—my sock penis was on full display. It was the last image Gia had of me.

After the ménage á disaster, I tried contacting Gia a thousand times. All of my efforts were a bust. It reached a point where all the Gia-adjacent connections I reached out to dodged me like I was a Jehovah's Witness. Hell, I wanted to slam the door in my own face.

I was stuck in a stalemate of rumination and regret and wasn't okay. I kept replaying the Alfred Hitchcock wet dream at Mimi's apartment and scratching my head. What happened? How could this be the outcome for Gia and me? Too many fries had been shared between us.

But most importantly, it wasn't my fault.

I tried to give myself some grace and Gia space to process. But her avoidance wasn't sitting right with me. Something had to happen to make Gia leave me in that apartment drugged, naked, and violated without so much as a goodbye or checking that I made it home safely.

Was she in shock? Did seeing me with my junk stuffed in a sock suddenly make me unlovable?

There was so much I didn't understand and needed to. I get the situation wasn't something you discussed without an overreach into some risky business. It's hard to imagine offering empathy and a cookie for our Eyes Wide Shut-like fiasco. Hell, I barely believed it myself. It definitely wasn't the white picket fence I'd signed up for. However, both of us were victims. And you're supposed to love the one you're with—flaws and all. But no one discusses what happens when the warts and all defense is having second thoughts about first impressions.

After a while, I realized there was time and space, and there was disregard. Gia's disappearing act leaned heavily towards disregard. I knew she'd been in contact with her family. Gia's father spilled the beans after I knocked on his door, looking like I'd been fighting with a flock of seagulls. And although she hadn't shared any details with them, it didn't make the slap of her avoidance sting any less. If anything, the shun registered somewhere between adolescent and abusive. I didn't deserve it. I didn't deserve any of it. But Gia had made her choice. Now, it was time for me to make mine.

I moved to DC to save myself from my own subconscious. I needed something that wasn't a woman to rebound me out of the Twilight Zone I'd experienced. I'd had enough of relationships and disrespect for several lifetimes. So, when I received a reporter job offer from USA Today, I took it. I'd interviewed for the job before Gia and I got engaged, and the timing of the offer couldn't have been better. I needed a clean slate. So, I buried my skeletons with Gia, packed up my life, moved to Washington, DC, and never looked back—until now.

Looking in the rearview mirror, Gia taught me a lot. For one, love and relationships are an interesting choice paradigm. A nuanced coin flip of uncontrolled variables. If you choose relationship and love, nothing is predictable. If you decide not to love or have a relationship, then everything is possible. But if the unexpected happens and then falls apart, you often have to heal twice. I'm not so sure healing again will be easier this time around.

*****************************************************************************

# PART 3
# The Facts of Life

## Elevator Pitch

COVID put flesh around the Grim Reaper and gave it multiple personalities: isolation, job loss, financial hardship, breakups, the essential worker facade... Yet, putting a face with the name hasn't satisfied the grief. Instead, it's brought an insecurity and sense of loss we haven't encountered before. Processing too much and gone too soon in rapid succession. Struggling to find footing in things that happen for many reasons and just because. We're trapped in a lousy fortune cookie prediction holding romanticized notions and a side of tragic implications.

Spring forward can kiss my ass! Whoever said time heals all wounds never experienced daylight savings during a pandemic. It's like suffering through involuntary jet lag and a hangover. Like my first marriage, you go through it but wish you hadn't.

Right now, all I want is coffee and the hour I lost. Unfortunately, I'll have to settle for one out of two. The only silver lining is my car clock being right again and not having to play for Sunday morning service. You have to take the wins where you can get them.

One thing I do know is that my circadian rhythm has a wicked sense of humor. For the past few weeks, I've been having this recurring dream. I wouldn't call it a nightmare, but it's definitely a slumber fuck.

Strangely, I had the dream three times last night. In the first two dreams, I'm in an unfamiliar building, trying to get to the fourth floor, but I can't figure out the damn elevators. I hop on one, and it takes me to the opposite side of the building. I jump in another, and it ushers me to the wrong floor. And just when I think I've got it figured out, I get on an elevator that spins uncontrollably. Round and round, zigzagging, shifting directions on this invisible track to God-knows-the-fuck-where. The inside of the elevator is glass with a blue carpet that's seen better days. I can see trees outside, the elevator button flashing for the fourth floor, and my fat ass getting tossed around for what seems like an eternity. Finally, the elevator stops. I get off, face a new row of elevator doors, and play the whole game of elevator roulette again. I never reach the fourth floor.

Now, in the third dream, I push the UP button and wait for the elevator. When it opens, Bones is in his boxers, holding hands with a skeleton. He's smiling like a jackal while the skeleton rests its head on his shoulder. I look at the skeleton, which is wearing a pair of skull and crossbone socks. After an awkward pause, the elevator doors close. I reach out to hit the UP button again, but before my finger touches the console, I see a sign above it that reads: FOURTH FLOOR.

I'm unable to fall back to sleep after the third dream. It's Sunday morning. Daylight's been saved but not baptized, and I figure the Father, Son, and Holy Ghost are giving me a subliminal heads-up. I can't say I'm keen on discovering what, though. I'm just hoping the revelation wasn't in that lost hour of sleep.

My caffeine fix hasn't kicked in enough to play Freud with my dream analysis, so I take my coffee outside on the porch to clear my head. When I step outside, I see one of the neighbor kids bouncing a basketball and blowing snot rockets. The scene was pure birth control. Johnny Snot Rocket was attempting a layup when my cell phone rang. It was Calvin FaceTiming me.

"Man, this week has been ten days! You think we saved too much daylight?" Calvin dove in, as usual, without a hello.

"Glad to see you've joined the tech era, Jailhouse Rock. When did you learn to FaceTime?" I asked.

"One of my grandkids showed me. I'm tired of all these masks, man. I need to see these females' faces before I bless them," Calvin said with attitude.

"Why is your decrepit behind out here trying to get some ass during a pandemic? You got a death wish?" I gave Calvin a look.

"Naw, man. I'm single, and a lotta these females got daddy issues. I'm just filling a void during these unprecedented times." Calvin made a vulgar hand gesture and laughed.

"Looks like you filling the hell outta that tiny ass shirt you're wearing. Damn, what have you been eating?" I gave him a quizzical glance. "Fuck the freshman 15. You messed around and gained the COVID 19!" I chuckled at my own joke.

"Whatever, punk ass! You just mad because your shirt looks like it needs Botox. What'd you do, iron it with a rock? And for your information, things expand when they heat up. I'm not fat; I'm hot. You need to brush up on your science." Calvin smiled into the camera as if he'd just dropped some Neil DeGrasse Tyson knowledge on me.

"I keep forgetting you're a descendant of the crack era. My bad, Heat Miser. So why you mean mugging me on a Sunday morning? I know you need prayer, but this is early, even for you."

"You need to get your people, dawg. These church folk out here wildin' out. Cedric's been having virtual worship services with the Praise Team, and they ALL got COVID. Man, the praises went up, and COVID came down. It's a mess. Everybody's doing okay, but keep them in your prayers." Calvin was shaking his head.

"Are you serious? Sounds like they need prayer for more than just COVID. That's proof that common sense isn't so common. Why do church folk believe being saved gives them immunity against a plague?" It was my turn to shake my head. "Thanks for telling me. I'll call Cynthia later and check on Cedric." I put a reminder on my phone while Calvin kept talking.

"Oh, and you remember that girl your first wife April used to hang with, Gia? Well, she caught COVID and died a few days ago. They're having a virtual memorial for her on Thursday." I stopped typing and looked back into the phone's camera.

"Wait, what did you say?" I asked Calvin.

"Gia died from COVID a few days ago. There's a memorial for her on Facebook Live this Thursday," Calvin repeated.

"Shit," I whispered. "Gia? April's Gia? Are you sure? You better not be playing with me! I mean...wow! I can't believe it. Wow..." I was utterly dumbfounded and kept repeating myself, trying to make sense of it. How could the past reappear and vanish simultaneously?

Calvin was still talking. I laid the phone in my lap and watched Johnny Snot Rocket tie his sneakers. I thought about the last time I saw Gia. It was at April's funeral. The irony made me shiver.

"Mylo! Yo, Mylo! Motherfucker, you still there?" Calvin's voice jolted me back to the present.

"Sorry!" I yelled and fumbled to pick up my phone. "Sorry, the news about Gia hit me sideways. It's one thing to hear about COVID taking out celebrities you grew up with. But Gia? Shit, that's REAL." I let out a huge breath and smoothed a palm over my head.

"I mean, this is *literally* burying a piece of my past. Is this what old age feels like, Calvin? 'Cause all of a sudden, I feel like a fossil." I stared at Calvin. He shrugged and stared back.

"Fuck this shit! I'm not adding this year to my age," Calvin announced. "I'm serious, Mylo! Life's outta control, so I'm taking something back. The only thing you can do about getting older is lie about it. And you know I can lie my ass off! Dammit, Imma be immortal!" Calvin beat his fist on his chest. I was cracking up.

"Calvin, don't ever change. You know, it's strange not having a funeral for Gia. COVID took that from us, too. Damn, we can't even grieve normally anymore."

I took a moment of silence.

"You watching the memorial?" I asked.

"Nope, flowers and Facebook scare me," Calvin shot back.

"Apparently, condoms do, too. Aren't you tired of having kids? *That's* what's immortalizing your horny ass! You need to leave those daddy-issue women alone. Shit, you're probably responsible for half the population of Buffalo by now. Haven't you proved enough?" I was laughing uncontrollably.

"Ha, ha, shut the fuck up. I'm not taking advice from someone who graduated from the Montessori School of Marriage," Calvin returned.

"Fool, can you spell Montessori?" I yelled. We both fell out laughing.

"Whatever! Your saditty ass. You probably put your pinky up when you fart. Remember, there's no supply chain shortage on a six-pack of whoop-ass," Calvin declared.

"Listen, I gotta go. I don't have time for your lip flapping. I've got some confused women who need my counsel." Calvin wiggled his eyebrows for emphasis.

"Love you, man. Be safe." Calvin disconnected the FaceTime call.

I wiped tears from the corners of my eyes from all the laughter. "Typical Calvin," I whispered before going into the house.

## Curtain Call

Gia's gone. I didn't know what to do with that information. No matter how often I turned the words over in my head, they still didn't register. I keep telling myself it's a defense mechanism or confirmation of my wife's theory that Hooked on Phonics didn't work for me. If nothing else, I sincerely hope someone nominates Gia for sainthood. Between her whacked-out family and... well, April, she at least deserves an honorable mention.

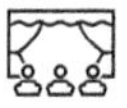

It's been nearly 20 years since I last saw Gia, but damn, *tomorrow isn't promised* didn't need to hit *this* hard. I truly admired Gia. Honestly, she was the only thing I liked about April. Now, all I have are memories, and I honestly don't know what to do with that.

To try and cope, I walked around the house examining things. For some reason, I found it calming. My feet paused on the carpet, then the hardwood. Watching dust filter through the light streaming from the windows. Hearing the breath in my ears as I stared at objects I was surrounded by every day but was just now noticing. It seemed odd initially, but now I realize I'm at peace. I also realize my damn coffee is cold. So I walk to the kitchen to dump it out. As I'm rinsing out the cup, I hear my wife, Traci, calling from upstairs.

"Mylo! Can you come up here for a moment? I need your opinion."

I placed the cup on the counter and walked upstairs. Traci was in the bedroom rearranging things. Since the pandemic hit, she'd practically rearranged the whole house. Our bedroom had managed to go unscathed—until now. She'd taken the curtains down and held two different panels up when I walked in.

"Which do you like better, the winter gray or the buttered rum?" she asked.

"I have no idea what any of that means. But if you're asking which color I like better, I'll take the blue." I responded.

Traci walked over and kissed me on the cheek. I guess I'd chosen right.

I stood in the doorway while Traci fiddled with more curtain paraphernalia. She had the radio on in the background. I hadn't noticed it when I came in, but now I heard Nick Gilder's *Hot Child in the City* playing. I got a chill. It was Gia's favorite song.

"What's wrong, Sweet Cheeks?" Traci asked. I hated the pet name, but hearing Traci say it made my heart smile.

"Huh? Oh, nothing," I finally responded. "The song on the radio's got me reminiscing about my Buffalo days, that's all. You want some help putting up the curtains?" I needed to divert my attention away from the song.

I walked over to the radio and changed the station before grabbing one of the curtain panels.

Traci and I stepped back to observe our handy work a few minutes later.

"Not too shabby, Mrs. Gunn! You should be on one of those budget make-over shows on HGTV or something. Who knew a color change could alter the whole vibe in here. I'm feeling it!" I wasn't blowing smoke. Traci had an amazing eye for anything artistic. I'd definitely married up.

Speaking of eyeing... I looked over and saw something on the bed that I hadn't noticed before.

"Hey, T, were you praying for an answer about the curtains before you called me up here?" I asked.

"What are you talking about?" Traci raised an eyebrow at me.

"The Bible over there on the bed. Where did it come from?" I probed.

"Oh, yeah. I found it while I was looking for the curtains. I think it might be yours."

Traci started moving throw pillows around. I went and picked up the Bible.

It was a wedding gift from Gia. I don't know why, but I took the Bible into the hallway and texted Bones.

*"Hey, Bones! Want to meet up at the field to blow off some steam? Today's been rough."*

Bones gave me a thumbs-up emoji and typed, *"See you in 30."*

I arrived at the field before Bones and sat in the stands. For once, the quiet felt good. I let my thoughts drift, closed my eyes, and exhaled.

A few moments later, I heard someone jogging up the steps to join me. When I opened my eyes, Bones stared at me like I was mutating another nose.

"What's wrong?" I asked. "I got a loose booger or something?" I wiped my nose and scanned myself for irregularities.

"Dude, you said you were having a rough day. But you're sitting here like the Dalai Lama at a silent retreat. What gives?" Bones was examining my face, looking for clues.

"Thanks for calling me Dalai Lama instead of Buddha," I chuckled. "I can't take any more sucker punches today." I stared at the houses surrounding the field and wondered what the people inside of them were doing.

Bones tapped me on the shoulder, and I turned to face him.

"Are you okay?" Bones was patting down my arm. "You look like Top Gun, but you're acting like an alien cult has abducted you. We don't need to change the podcast story, do we? Please tell me you're not communicating with E.T.'s second cousin. Talk to me, bro." Bones was joking, but his concern was genuine.

"You need to take that crazy imagination of yours down a few pegs. I'm fine, I think. And no, we don't need to change the story. I'm just experiencing my first COVID casualty," I confessed.

"Oh, wow! I'm so sorry for your loss. Was it someone close to you?"

"Somewhat. It was April's former best friend, Gia. They grew up across the street from one another and were inseparable through adulthood. I called them Siamese Twins. Where you saw one, you saw the other." I chuckled at the memory.

"Gia was the maid of honor at our wedding. But she and April had parted ways when I came home from my first overseas military assignment. I never found out why." I paused to bat away a bug, trying to get my attention.

"The last time I saw Gia was at *April's* funeral. Now she's gone, too. I can't explain it, but learning of her death has given me a sense of relief." I looked at my running shoes and tented my fingers.

"I get it. You just lost your last link to April. It's understandable why that would make you exhale. The two of them probably put you through a lot if they were joined at the hip." Bones chimed in.

"Actually, Gia was the best thing about April. If I'd been smart, I would have dumped April and dated Gia instead. Boy, she used to let April have it, too! Gia didn't take ANY shit from April! It was poetic to watch how she handled her. I'm sure the first thing Gia did when she got through the pearly gates was to find April and punch her in the face. She was 135 pounds of curls and attitude. All the Mazzas are tough as nails." I professed.

"Wait, Gia's last name was Mazza?" Bones asked.

"Yeah, I keep forgetting you're from Buffalo, too. Did you know any Mazzas? They were a BIG Italian family..."

Bones interjected. "Sorry, bro, but did April have a nickname by any chance?" Bones' voice was shaky.

"Yeah, her family and close friends called her Mimi. I never liked calling her that, though. Sounds like someone who eats cucumber sandwiches and has a sister named Muffy. I wasn't down with it. Why'd you ask?"

I looked at Bones. He got up and started walking down the stairs.

"Bones! What's wrong? Did I say something out of pocket?" I yelled after him.

"No. I'm fine. You didn't... Listen, I just remembered that I've got something urgent to do for work. No rest for the wicked on a crime podcast." Bones was hustling to get away and left his workout bag.

I tried to get his attention, but he kept moving and never turned around. I watched him trot toward the parking lot. "Bones is running from something," I said to myself.

Since it looked like I wouldn't get what I came to the field for, I got up and walked to my car. When I got to the parking lot, I saw Bones' car was still there. I went over and tapped on the window.

"Jesus! You scared the piss outta me!" Bones screamed.

"Roll down the window," I directed. "You're not a Mickey D's drive-thru."

Bones put the window down.

"You left your gym bag, Speedy Gonzales." I held up the bag and handed it to Bones. "Why are you still sitting here? You okay?" I asked.

Bones let out a big sigh and put his forehead on the steering wheel."My car won't start! The stupid car won't start!" Bones slammed his hands on the dashboard, then smashed the start button several times to prove his point.

"Okay, man. Calm down; it's not the end of the world. Do you have AAA or some other service we can call?"

Bones put his forehead back on the steering wheel. "I've got AAA," he murmured. He grabbed his gym bag and ruffled through it. Then he started throwing the contents onto the seat. "Are you kidding me? Really? I left my wallet at the house! Dammit!" Bones threw the gym bag at the passenger seat window and started crying.

I opened the car door.

"Bones, get out of the car," I said calmly.

Bones hid his face in his hands.

"Get out of the car, Bones. It's not like you're going anywhere. I'll take you home so you can call AAA. I got you, bro."

Bones stepped out of the car. I ushered him over to the stairs and told him to sit down. I joined him a few feet away.

"Something tells me this has nothing to do with your car not starting," I expressed.

"Now look who's trying to be Dr. Phil." Bones quipped and grinned. "But you're right, it isn't, and you're not gonna like what it's about."

"Hey, we both know I'm the Grinch who hates everything. So you've got nothing to lose. Hit me with your best shot. You've already dubbed me the Dalai Lama."

Bones sighed heavily and turned his head in the opposite direction.

I could tell he needed space, so I went to my car. When I came back, I handed Bones a beer.

"I had a feeling we'd need these. It's probably warm, but it'll do the trick." I handed Bone's a bottle opener. He opened the beer and chugged half the bottle.

"Damn, man! Let me get a few sips in before you let loose. Wanna make sure we're functioning on the same level." I opened my beer, took a few swallows, and sat down.

"Okay. Whew! All right." Bones nervously picked his beer up and put it down several times. "Look, Top Gun, you better sit a few more feet away from me. I may need a head start." Bones instructed.

I scooted over a few feet and took another swig of beer.

"There's no delicate way to say this, so I'll be direct. Straight, no chaser. Okay, here goes... I fucked April." Bones slid over to the stair railing and looked at me.

"What did you just say?" I reacted.

"You heard me correctly. I had sex with April. Probably while you two were married. Let me explain before you beat my brakes off." Bones hugged the railing while I put down my beer.

"I'm listening," I responded.

"In my defense, I didn't know April was married. She was living with this guy, Chad. Oh my God! Chad! That's the dude she cheated on you with! Jesus, this is so bizarre!" Bones ran his hand through his hair and gave me a pensive glance. "Sorry, I'm rambling." Bones took a deep breath.

"Gia was my fiancé then and the only woman I've ever loved. When Gia and I announced our engagement, April wigged out. She set up this whole situation. Told me she was hosting an engagement party. Instead, she drugged me, forced me to have a threesome with her and Gia's sister, Noemi, and conveniently arranged for Gia to walk in on us during the act. It was awful. I was so messed up that I went into the kitchen and made a sandwich while April and Gia duked it out. April told Gia she was her soulmate and wanted to spend the days she had left with her. Then she told Gia to dump me because I was in the way.

Gia spit in April's face and left me butt naked in the kitchen, holding a sandwich with a sock covering my junk. That was the last time I saw or spoke to Gia. I moved to DC shortly after that." Bones loosened his grip on the railing and turned to the side.

I started laughing. "Shit! So you're telling me you dropped trough, took a bow, and Gia left your ass holding a sandwich and your manhood in a sock? That's pretty fucked up." Now I was laugh-talking. "Tell me. The sock on your junk, did it have a skull and crossbones?"

"Yeah, how did you know?" Bones asked, puzzled.

I laughed even harder. Freud was having a field day with me.

"Dude, you know how women's periods sync up after they start hanging out for a while? Don't ask me how I know this, but I think you and I might have the male equivalent," I answered.

Bones looked at me like I'd just told him 1+1=8.

"Bones, you really need to let go of that railing before you have to buy it dinner and an IUD. I promise I'm not gonna do anything to you." I chuckled and moved closer to Bones to see if he'd run. He didn't.

We sat in silence for several minutes. I could hear Bones breathing like he was about to have an asthma attack. He didn't have asthma, so I broke the silence to keep him from hyperventilating.

"Hey, Bones."

He turned to look at me, still leaning against the railing.

"Was it me, or was Noemi's tongue double-jointed?"

The look on Bone's face was priceless.

"I can tell by your expression that that's exactly what you thought I'd say." I quipped. "Listen, you weren't the only one who had a Pill Cosby moment with my former wife. April did that same shit to me and called it an apology for cheating with Chad. So yeah, I'm not surprised to learn there were more victims of her sick sense of entitlement. April was a cold-blooded monster. I'm really sorry she hurt you and Gia."

I held my fist out to Bones for a pound. He inched away from the railing and obliged.

"I'm sorry, Top Gun," Bones gushed. "I completely Single White Femaled your grief and poured gasoline on the fire. You must think I'm some heartless goon." he put his face in his hands again.

"Bones, if you start crying again, I swear I'll kick your ass," I said calmly.

Bones moved his hands from his face. I gave him a look that let him know I wasn't playing.

"So, what do we do now?" Bones asked.

"We both need another beer." I got up and walked back to my car.

## Six Degrees of Separation

For the next three hours, Bones and I swapped stories about Gia.

I told Bones about seeing Gia at April's funeral and meeting her husband. They'd gotten married the year before and spent their honeymoon in Vietnam.

Bones relayed the first time he met Gia and her question about dogs in Vietnam that made him fall in love with her. He was glad she'd remembered Vietnam and wished he could ask her if she tried sautéed poodle.

We reminisced about french fries, fist fights, and Gia's unorthodox, independent personality. We pondered how funny and cunning, and curious Gia was. Then, the discussion turned to Gia's benevolence and mystery with April. It was a "did they, didn't they" debate on whether April and Gia were secretly a couple. I shared April's Pearl Harbor incident to settle the debate. We agreed that April and Gia were more than Siamese Twins.

There was all this hidden history between Bones and me. For decades, I believed I was a prisoner of my subjective experience. Now, I learned I had a cellmate and a new perspective on shared experiences. We had a lot to unpack. As April said, people need people. And Bones and I had some collective healing to do. His writing prompts hadn't triggered me to mention Gia in my journal. But this new revelation was bound to spice up the podcast production.

After running out of stories and bottle caps, Bones and I decided to call it a day. We still had to get Bones's car towed. Bones helped me discard the beer bottles, and we walked to my car.

"Bones, you gotta mask?" I asked. "If not, Imma need you to sit in the back seat, roll down the window, and stick your head out. It's only a five-minute drive. Just be careful not to swallow any bugs."

"Why don't I drink a bottle of Purell since I'm already halfway drunk? And for your information, five minutes is a long time in dog years since you're treating me like a wayward cocker spaniel," Bones jabbed back.

"Look, we just lost the love of your life and my ex-wife's side piece to COVID. And while this trip down memory lane has been the highlight of my day, I'm not trying to meet the Siamese Twins in the afterlife anytime soon. So mask up or go doggy style. Your choice." I put on my mask and got in the car.

"Unlock the backseat, jackass!" Bones yelled.

I drove 20 miles an hour and took the scenic route to his house.

Bones blew a humungous fart inside the car before closing the door. Our friendship was now official.

*************************************************************************************

JODY PASCHAL

# Closure

## Collateral Damage

# Pitch Perfect and Off-Key

Preparing for this podcast has been pitch-perfect and off-key. That's not a complaint, just an observation. I'm a musician, so I tend to experience nuance differently. At first, I was journaling away my angst without any structure. Then Bones came along, put me in a trench coat, and helped me look for my grip on reality.

Now, I've made peace with being an inconvenient truth: I was groomed. Tricked by sexual platitudes into a marriage where I was a chore on a managed care to-do list for a woman whose pet peeves were monogamy and kindness. Yes, that's a mouthful. But it's easier said than bean-counting emotional scars to justify reality. The reality is that some people walk through the world with an unimpeachable morality; the rest of us are just collateral damage. It is what it is.

I finally finished my last journal entry for Bones. It took me an entire month to write. Not because I didn't know what to say, but for what *had* to be said. Writing about being groomed may have been easier if I'd been lured to an early bird dinner by some gnarled-knuckled old hag. But April was young and beautiful. She just happened to have an agenda that left me with the short end of the stick.

I know that's not unique or special. I consider myself lucky under the circumstances. However, I'm now realizing that it's not the memories that haunt you; it's the years you can't undo.

I'm not bitter, though; I'm better. I've realized that "love" takes an ass whoopin' when "like" isn't around to support it. So, I've learned how to like. My wife, Traci, and I are best friends. It was our friendship that led to marriage, not micro-dosing happiness through sex. That's the lesson learned when the sheets were rough in the last bed you made.

Looking back, I don't know how I survived the strain of being around a wife whose actions I couldn't tolerate all those years. It took a while to get down from that high horse. Now, I have a loving wife who takes a nap when she gets tired of me instead of masterminding other people's demise.

By the way, I did return to Dr. Ruffin to help me deal with April. I stuck to my guns and opted against divorce threats. But I protected my peace and assets by filing for legal separation and living in my own apartment for the duration of our marriage. I stayed with April for the last few months of her life. The relationship was medically transactional then, and I don't regret the decision.

After April died, my whole perspective on life changed. I discovered real love with Traci, settled down in Washington, DC, and felt comfortable in my own skin for the first time. I was a better person without April. Ans now, at 50, I'm growing into myself again. I'll admit, the growing pains don't suck as much this time around. But they're still no picnic. At first, I thought that turning 50 and the pandemic had turned the clock back on all my progress. Now, I know it's just a reminder of how far I've come.

## Pass the Dutchie

I texted Bones to let him know I'd finished my final journal prompt and offered to drop it off at his place. He told me that wouldn't be a good idea. His landlord went off her lithium, so he and her poor husband had to deal with her real personality (which wasn't pretty). I said I understood and would wait for him on my front porch.

Bones arrived 20 minutes later. I handed him the journal and an Arnold Palmer. He thanked me for both, and we sat in silence for a bit. I was beginning to enjoy silence more now that my thoughts were clearer.

"Bones, can I ask you a personal question?" I broke the silence.

"Sure, you've smelled my farts, so there's not much else to hide."

We both snickered.

"Why have you remained a bachelor all these years? Didn't you ever want to find love again after Gia?" I inquired.

"Whoa! You meant *really* personal! Well, I've boned your wife, and we both banged my almost sister-in-law. So I suppose this is my penance." Bones crossed his ankle over his knee and put his hands behind his head.

"So, as you can imagine, I developed some pretty heavy trust issues after what happened with Gia. Until a few weeks ago, I'd never had any closure to the relationship. I guess I've carried that unprocessed grief around with me all these years. As a result, I've harbored this constant feeling that my future is off and my judgment of women is broken. So, I've lived life with the motto, "You can't get hurt if you're never in a relationship." I like to think I'm the kind of guy who's whole on his own." Bones moved his hands to his knee and leaned forward.

"I couldn't get past the fact that Gia would leave me without so much as a conversation or a goodbye. Since then, relationships, for me, have become a loop of tragic implications or settling for no one. I've chosen the latter." Bones nodded his head.

"Thanks for sharing that with me. Hurt is always the third wheel in relationships. I totally get it. There was a time when a woman even mentioned a relationship to me, I wished I had a gun. But now look at me. I'm the poster child of marital domesticity."

We both laughed.

"Hold tight. I'll be right back." I got up and went into the house. I returned holding the Bible that Gia had given me.

Bones glanced at the Bible and held his hands up. "Listen, you can save your breath. I already know He dies in the end."

"Shut up you heathen!" I tossed the Bible on Bones' lap and sat down.

"I want you to read the inside cover, then open the card. I'm going inside to grab a lighter and something stronger than iced tea."

I went into the house to give Bones some privacy.

Bones smoothed his hand over the Bible before opening it to read the inside cover.

*Mylo,*

*I'm so happy you're marrying my best friend. But a word of caution. You're gonna need to stay on your knees for this one.*

*God Bless Your Mess!*

*Gia*

Bones closed his eyes and smiled. He took a few deep breaths and took the card out of the envelope. The front of the card read:

*Just wanted to send you some sunshine during this trying time.*

Bones broke out laughing and opened the card to see the original message was blacked out. In its place, Gia wrote:

*You're gonna need some extra blunts for this shit. Don't smoke it all at once!*

*Love ya!*
*Gia*

The card envelope also contained an untouched marijuana cigarette.

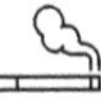

When Mylo returned from inside the house, Bones was holding the blunt between his fingers. Mylo placed a bottle of Hennessey and two shot glasses on the table. Then he sat down, poured two shots, and handed one to Bones.

"I take it you read the assignments," Mylo asked Bones.

Bones nodded and saluted with the joint still between his fingers.

"Excellent, my friend." Mylo settled in his seat and turned towards Bones. "Gia gave me that Bible the day April and I got married. She gave me the card after we got engaged. Now, I'm giving them both to you."

A tear rolled down Bones' cheek.

"I can't accept this, bro. You need—"

Mylo cut Bones off. "Bones, your taking this helps us both. I need to release April, and you need closure with Gia. I thing this will help with the process.

Bones turned his hands in a prayer pose and whispered, "Thank you."

"Okay, now for a toast! Raise your glass." Mylo stood up with the shot glass in his hand.

"To April, Gia, and Noemi's acrobatic tongue! Love can't all be opioids and threesomes. Salud!" Mylo downed his shot.

Bones followed suit.

"Now, let's fire up that blunt. You think it's still good after 30 years?" Mylo took the lighter out of his pocket and flicked it on.

Bones held out the blunt and shrugged his shoulders.

"Guess we'll find out. Puff, puff, pass!" Mylo yelled.

THE END

Groomed |

# About the Author

**JODY PASCHAL** is a first-time novelist addicted to storytelling and sarcasm. This book is the brainchild of a need to be a humorous voice amplifier for unspoken taboos.

www.ingramcontent.com/pod-product-compliance
Lightning Source LLC
Chambersburg PA
CBHW062140110525
26522CB00008B/415
*9798227679055*